LOVE IN FOCUS

LOVE IN FOCUS

J.S. Young

LoveSong Publishing

LOVE IN FOCUS

LoveSong Publishing

ISBN: 979-8-218-90671-9

First Edition: 2026

Printed in the United States of America

For those who thought soft love wasn't for them—
until it was

Prologue

Three Years Ago

Amara Jones wasn't the kind of woman people
noticed when she walked into a room. She knew
what worked for her and stuck to what felt right.
But tonight, standing in her apartment getting
ready for her birthday party with the help of her
best friends Sadie, Kelsie and Rebekah, she felt
beautiful. Radiant, even.

Born on Valentine's Day to parents who
were practically shot by Cupid, Amara had always
romanticized her birthday. So much so that her
birthday parties had been affectionately dubbed
the Cupid Bashes.

"Okay, turn again," Sadie instructed, stepping back with a critical eye. "Let me see that slit in motion."

Amara twirled. The rose-gold sequins of her custom gown caught the light, the thigh-high slit revealing a glimpse of her honey-toned leg. The deep V neckline made her feel sensual and confident. This year's Cupid Bash was extra special, thrown by her long-term boyfriend Marcus.

"Whew, Marcus is gonna lose his mind," Kelsie said with a low whistle.

"He better," Amara said, fluffing her curls.

"The man rented the nicest rooftop in Midtown, hired a full band of violinists, invited all your people? Babe, this might be proposal night."

Amara laughed, giddy. "You think so?"

"Oh! For sure!" Sadie said, adding one final swipe of gloss to Amara's lips.

Across the room, Rebekah sat on the edge of the sofa, twisting a dread between her fingers. She was unusually quiet.

"You okay?" Amara asked, smiling at her reflection in the mirror.

Rebekah blinked and forced a smile. "Yeah. I'm good. Just... excited for you. I'm gonna head to the venue and make sure everything's running smoothly."

"You sure? We can all ride together."

"Nah," Rebekah said quickly. "I'll catch you there."

She was gone before anyone could stop her.

An hour later, the rooftop lounge pulsed with energy. Rose petals blanketed the floor. Candles flickered in tall hurricane vases. A string quartet played R&B covers. Everyone Amara loved was there, raising glasses in her honor. And Marcus? He hadn't left her side all night.

He looked like a dream in a tailored burgundy suit, his warm brown skin glowing under the blush lighting. He leaned down, his cologne wrapping around her like a promise.

"You happy, birthday girl?" he murmured.

Amara leaned into him. "So happy."

She had never been more sure of him and their inevitable future together. The doors slammed open, stealing the attention of the whole room. Heads turned. The quartet went silent.

"Amara!" Rebekah slurred. She stood in the doorway barefoot, heels in her hand, mascara streaking her cheeks.

"Bekah?" Amara stepped forward. She could feel her heart fluttering in her throat. "What's wrong? Are you okay?"

"I'm sorry," Rebekah whispered. "I didn't mean for it to happen. I swear, I didn't."

Amara's stomach flipped. "Didn't mean for what to happen?"

Rebekah's eyes jolted between her and Marcus, guilt trembling through her voice. "Marcus and I," she swallowed hard, "we've been sleeping together... for months."

A ringing filled Amara's ears. The room spun as her brain scrambled to translate what her friend had said.

"What?" she whispered, voice cracking as reality snapped into place.

Marcus face drained of color.

"What the hell are you talking about!?" he said, voice unsteady. He grabbed Amara's hand, and

4

looked straight into her eyes, pleading. "Baby, she's drunk. I don't know what she's saying."

Rebekah let out a bitter laugh, eyes wild.

"You lying son of a—" She lunged at him, slapping him so hard the sound ricocheted across the rooftop. Gasps rippled through the room.

"Tell her the truth!" she screamed. "Tell her how you said you were lonely since her career took off. How you were out 'recruiting' players when you were actually taking weekend vacations with me. Or how you left her bed in the middle of the night to crawl into mine!"

The room tilted. Her hands shook so hard she nearly dropped her glass. Marcus reached for her as whispers rippled around them.

"Amara, please. Don't listen to her. She's spiraling. I would never do that. I would never hurt you." His voice cracked, but she couldn't tell if it was desperation or guilt.

She stood there frozen. In the middle of what she believed would be an engagement. How did such a beautiful night turn into her worse nightmare delivered by the two people she loved and trusted the most? Everything she believed in was cracking beneath her feet. She didn't even notice Sadie and Kelsie joining her at her side.

"Tell me this is a sick joke," Sadie said sharply.

Marcus hung his head.

"I'm sorry, Mar," he whispered. "I fucked up."

Kelsie stepped forward and clapped once. Hard.

"Alright! Party's over. Everyone OUT."

The room evacuated fast. Nobody tested Kelsie's voice when she used that tone. Sadie stepped right into Marcus's chest, all five foot two of her radiating fury. She shoved him.

"Go cheat in traffic."

His jaw tensed, but he obliged. Rebekah stood close behind, trembling. "I didn't want to hurt you."

Sadie snapped. "Bitch, you better get your ass outta here before I beat it for Amara. You are no friend of hers."

Amara's voice was soft but steady. "You may not have meant to, Bek, but there's no coming back from this."

♥

Later that night, Amara, Sadie and Kelsie sat on the floor of Amara's apartment. Their gowns were gone, replaced by oversized sweatpants and hoodies. Bacon cheeseburgers and fries from their favorite spot, Ronnie's sat on the coffee table next to two chilled bottles of champagne. Kelsie poured the bubbly into their mismatched coffee mugs.

"Eat, babe," she said, handing Amara a burger. "Your heart's broken, but your stomach shouldn't suffer for it."

She lit a candle and put on the breakup playlist they made at Hilltop U.

"Why does it hurt so bad?" Amara whispered pulling her knees to her chest.

"Because you loved him," Sadie said, "and you didn't deserve this."

She glanced at her phone. "One minute to midnight."

Kelsie exhaled, then started singing.

"Happy birthday to you..."

Sadie joined in, loud and off-key.

"Happy birthday to you..."

Amara sniffled, a broken laugh slipping through her tears.

"Happy birthday, dear Amara..."

"Happy birthday to you..."

She raised her mug and clinked it against theirs. Her voice came out quiet but full of fire.

"To friends, to family, to love..."

She paused.

"You know what? Fuck love!"

Chapter One

Present Day

The sound of rain tapping against the oversized windows of her home library was one of the reasons Amara bought the modern ranch-style home tucked beneath Red Oak trees. The mosquitoes were ruthless in the summer, but in the fall? The place felt like something out of a moody indie movie.

She sat at her desk, hair twisted into a messy curly bun, tortoiseshell glasses perched on her nose. Lounging in her tan Hilltop University sweatshirt with matching biker shorts and knee-high socks. She sipped from her cream-colored Amara Designs tumbler and set it beside her laptop as she finished her video call.

"Yes, a minimalist boho-inspired loft area can definitely be done," she said with a warm smile.

Her friend had connected her with CeCe Hughes. Yes, *that* CeCe Hughes, wife of Major League Baseball MVP, Andre Hughes and not to mention, the star of Baseball Wives. She'd enlisted Amara to redesign the loft in their home and it took everything in her not to fangirl.

"Any personal touches you'd like me to add?"

Amara had been obsessed with interior design since childhood, always rearranging her room and adding flair to the family living room. Now, she was one of the most in-demand high-end interior designers in Atlanta.

"Great! I'll stop by next Thursday at eleven for a site visit. I'll bring reference photos from previous projects for inspiration. Can't wait to collaborate."

When the call ended, she checked the time, set her out-of-office reply and shut her laptop. Time for her weekly lunch with the girls. She showered, freed her curls from the bun, and slipped into her jeans with a nude turtleneck. She completed the look with gold hoops and soft brown lip gloss.

She grabbed her purse and slid into her metallic brown luxury SUV. Before pulling off, she opened the text thread affectionately titled Girls With the Tattoos. She and her friends had gotten matching rose tattoos one wild night in Vegas, and for a while, it defined them.

Amara:
OTW to the restaurant.
Lunch on me today!

Wednesday lunches were a tradition that had started in their Hilltop University Art History class. It didn't take long for it to become their mid-week therapy session. As their careers picked up, their busy schedules pushed lunch to 3 p.m. Early enough for a drink, late enough to still count as a workday.

Kelsie was already seated on the restaurant patio, glowing as always. The autumn sun kissed her mahogany skin, making heads turn as she scrolled through her phone. Her fresh silk press swung in the breeze, bone-straight and glossy.

Kelsie Black is a former runway model turned Editor-in-Chief of Royalty Magazine. She carried Hollywood roots and a reputation that stood on its own.

"Kels!" Amara grinned.

"Hello, beautiful," Kelsie responded, barely glancing up. "Your friend is late...AGAIN."

"You know Sadie moves to her own beat. And what does she always say?"

Together they mocked, "Time is subjective."

"Because it is!"

They turned to see Sadie approaching, impossible to miss.

"SADIE!"

Both women stood to hug her as if they hadn't seen each other at Sunday dinner.

Sadie Goodman was the freest spirit Amara knew. Petite, with long wavy sandy-brown hair, bright hazel eyes and freckles that lit her entire face. She dressed like a seventies rockstar and cared about no one's opinions. Her parents had met at a concert in the eighties and had been on a permanent road trip ever since. She and her twin brother Andie had been homeschooled across the country, *which* explained a lot.

"You could've at least ordered the vegan cheese sticks for me," Sadie complained.

"Literally nobody wants those," Kelsie groaned. "Where is that waiter with my Lemon Drop?!"

"He's probably bragging about serving The Kelsie Black," Amara teased.

"Well, he's blowing it."

They laughed as the waiter appeared with their drinks.

"Ah! My Lemon Drop. Thanks..." Kelsie squinted. "Tad."

"Yes ma'am." His voice cracked.

Kelsie gestured to her friends. "A Cosmo for her and whatever wheatgrass concoction you've got for that one."

"You know what?!" Sadie started.

"Kidding!" Kelsie said quickly. "A margarita and two orders of vegan cheese sticks for the table."

Sadie smirked. "I knew you liked them."

Kelsie rolled her eyes. "Okay, Amara. Spill. How was the date?"

Amara groaned. "A nightmare. Freddy Krueger actually would have made the date better."

She told them about his late arrival, the lack of manners, the open-mouth chewing. Her friends howled.

"Don't give up," Kelsie placed her hand on Amara's shoulder. "Dating is a numbers game."

"That's easy for you to say. You're Kelsie Black" Amara replied.

"And *you're* Amara Jones."

She rolled her eyes. "I deleted that Venus Dating App. I'm done. It's still Fuck Love over here."

"I keep telling you," Sadie said, "the universe sends your person when you least expect it."

"Here she goes with the universe again," Kelsie muttered.

Their bickering was routine, but their loyalty was unmatched. When Kelsie left modeling, tabloids dragged her. Sadie clapped back so hard she made Page Six. The paparazzo cried as Sadie looked unbothered in oversized sunglasses. Iconic.

"Enough about my sad dating life," Amara said. "Who's your latest victim, Kels?"

"They are not victims. They want to be here."

They laughed.

"Okay, but there is this one guy..." Kelsie said, tone shifting.

Sadie's eyes widened. "Wait. Do you actually like him?"

"She never likes them longer than three months," Amara added.

"It's science," Kelsie insisted. "People show their true colors after ninety days."

"Okay, Bill Nye," Sadie teased.

They swapped stories about work, celebrity clients and deadlines as they ate. When the check came, Kelsie cleared her throat and exchanged a look with Sadie.

Amara narrowed her eyes. "What are y'all scheming now?"

Sadie grinned. "We think it's time..."

"For you to bring back your Cupid Bash for your birthday!" Kelsie announced.

Amara blinked, her voice flat with exhaustion. "You know I don't do that anymore."

"We know," Sadie said gently. "But it's been three years."

Three years since Marcus. Her college sweetheart, President of his fraternity, the most successful sports agent in the city. On her twenty-seventh birthday, aka the very last Cupid Bash she would ever throw, her college roommate Rebekah had drunkenly confessed to sleeping with him. For months!

Kelsie and Sadie went into full protection mode. They shut the party down, dragged Marcus and Rebekah out, and held Amara while she cried. At midnight they convinced her to toast her birthday with shots, a bacon cheeseburger, fries and champagne. Everything changed for her that night. The future she thought she would have, her views of love, all skewed. The silver lining in all of this was her friendship deepening with Kelsie & Sadie, and distracted herself by pouring everything into building Amara Designs into what it is today.

"You're dating again, your business is booming and it's your thirtieth," Kelsie pressed. "Let's close your twenties out with a bang."

Sadie leaned in. "It's time to reintroduce the world to Amara."

"I mean..." Amara hesitated. "Five months isn't much time. A venue, invitations—"

"We'll take care of it," Kelsie cut in.

"With our connections? This will be the party of the year," Sadie added. "All we need is a yes."

Amara exhaled. "... sure."

Her friends squealed.

"Y'all are some bullies."

"It's all out of love!"

Amara smiled, though something inside her still felt unsure. The Cupid Bash was more than a party. It was a symbol of a past she didn't know she was ready to face again.

But maybe it was time to be brave.

Chapter Two

Since the breakup, Amara made it a priority to spend time with the people who truly mattered. Thursdays became her day for that. She wrapped up work early, changed into her barista look—jeans, a black shirt and a mocha-colored Jones Café hat—then headed over to help her parents close the shop.

She had three active clients. A proposal for a boutique hotel, a home staging for a longtime realtor, and next week's house visit with CeCe Hughes. Each client had a labeled file folder. She tucked fabric swatches inside and stuck Post-it notes wherever inspiration had hit. The soft sound of birdsong chimed from her phone. A text from her mom reminding her it was time to switch gears. Amara packed away her design materials and changed into her café clothes.

Smooth jazz played softly as she stepped through the single glass door of Jones Café. The crisp scent of new books made her want to curl up in a window chair and read the night away. The aroma of roasted hazelnuts and apple cinnamon pastries pulled her fully into the magic of the place.

"Cupcake!"

Her shoulders relaxed at her childhood nickname. At nine years old, she'd challenged the neighborhood kids to a cupcake-eating contest. She destroyed the competition and her stomach. Her mom had been furious, but her dad? He was proud. He stayed up all night nursing her back to health and crowned her "Cupcake." She hadn't eaten one since, but the name stuck.

Jerome Jones was a retired investor but looked every bit like a retired linebacker. Six foot five, 280 pounds, with a booming laugh and a magnetic presence. He lit up every room he walked into.

Her dad had one non-negotiable when it came to running the café. Close early on Thursdays and let someone else handle Sundays. That way, he never missed Thursday night football or Sunday games. The fact that church let out right before kickoff. Jerome called that divine timing.

"Hey, Dad." She hugged him tight. "Where's Mom?"

"She's in the back closing the kitchen. Said she's got something for you."

Knowing her mom, that could mean anything. Amara braced herself as she headed toward the back.

"Amara! Mon amour!" her mom sang in an over-the-top French accent as she twirled out of the kitchen.

Ashleigh Jones was a retired high school theater teacher who was forever in character.

"Really, Mom? We're Parisian today?"

"Why of course, mademoiselle. We brought out the apple cinnamon crepes for our fall special.

"Mom, please."

"No, no, no. En français."

"Sil vous plaît?" Amara tried.

"See!" The accent vanished, replaced by Ashleigh's native New Orleans drawl. "I knew those French lessons would pay off."

"Dad said you have something for me?"

Mrs. Jones crossed to the far side of the kitchen and returned with a medium-sized white box.

"I didn't want to open this without you." She slid it across the counter.

Amara opened it and squealed. "The new Brandi Hicks novel!"

Brandi Hicks was her favorite author, and the *Highway to Love* release had been on her calendar for months.

"I wanted you to have first dibs," her mom said with a smile.

Amara rushed around the island and hugged her, kissing her cheek. "Thank you. This just made my week."

Her mom paused, hearing the shift in her daughter's tone. "Everything okay, baby?"

"Yes. Everything's fine. The girls convinced me...well, strong-armed me into bringing back my Cupid Bash. I don't know if I'm ready."

Mrs. Jones gave her a soft, knowing look and pulled two stools over. *Here comes the TV mom moment*, Amara thought. Her mother took her hands.

"Sweetheart, what happened was traumatic, no doubt. But it's time to move on. You're stronger because of it, and you deserve to celebrate yourself. Throw the party. Enjoy it. Bring in your thirtieth the right way."

She stood and kissed the top of Amara's head. "Let us know how your dad and I can help."

"I will." Amara nodded. "What can I do to help close tonight?"

"Well," her mom pointed to the box, "you can start by putting those books on the shelf for me."

"Yes ma'am." Amara grabbed her apron and skipped out of the kitchen.

She headed to the romance section, arranging the books as the new Spotlight of the Month. While she perfected the display, she heard her mom at the counter, voice turned up a notch.

"Amara! Amara! Excuse me, I know she's here somewhere."

Oh no. That wasn't her mom's selling voice. That was her matchmaking voice.

Panic shot through her as she stacked the books a little too fast. There was no time to make the display pretty. She needed to escape. But it was too late.

A cool hand touched her arm.

"There you are."

"Hey, Mom," Amara said, trying to sound casual. "Did you need help with something else?"

Her mother leaned in closely, voice dropping so only Amara could hear. "There is a handsome, young, single man at the counter, and you'll never guess what he just ordered."

Amara lifted a brow, humoring her. "What did he order, Mom?"

"He ordered your coffee."

"What?" Amara blinked. "Nobody orders a brown sugar macchiato with macadamia milk and three extra espresso shots but me."

"That's what I thought. Until he did."

Before she could protest, Mrs. Jones tugged her toward the front.

"Ryan, was it?" her mom asked sweetly.

The mystery man nodded, smiling.

Amara rolled her eyes, then turned to fully face him.

Everything else blurred.

The man was fine. He towered over her, all six foot three of smooth deep-brown skin. Fresh low cut with deep waves, dimples for days. A beauty mark sat above his right dimple like punctuation on his perfect smile. His jawline could have been carved by Michelangelo, and that beard? Immaculate.

"Amara... Amara. Amaaaara," her mother sang, lightly shaking her out of her daze.

She flushed. Time to redeem herself. Act normal.

"Sorry. Um, hi. I'm Amara." *Nice.* "An apple cinnamon crepe would go perfectly with your coffee."

"Let's add one on, then," Ryan said, voice low and smooth. A Texas drawl coated his words just enough to charm the café owner's daughter.

He hadn't expected the owner's daughter to be this gorgeous.

Her natural curls framed her face like a halo, almost hiding her almond-shaped eyes.

"I'm also looking for a book," he added, clearing his throat.

"I can help you with that," she said, a little too quickly.

He leaned closer, the scent of bergamot and amber curling around her.

"I'm looking for..." he paused. "*Highway to Love.*"

She shot up straight. "By Brandi Hicks? She's my favorite author. I didn't take you for a Hickie."

Her face flamed.

Ryan lifted a brow.

"Uhm. That's what her fans call themselves. Hickies." She tugged at her sweater sleeve, still blushing.

He grinned. "I'm not sure I'm a Hickie, but I'm a photographer when I'm not loading up on caffeine and charming café owners' daughters."

She smiled. "Well, you're in luck. I just put the books out. You'll be the second copy sold today."

"Who bought the first?"

She pointed to herself.

Stunning and witty. That did it for him.

"Follow me," she said, leading him to the romance section. "So how did you end up shooting for Brandi?"

"My mom stayed wrapped in a quilt reading a book. Usually one with a shirtless guy holding a woman with their hair blowing in the wind."

She laughed. "The classics."

"Right. Photography's my thing, and after my mom died three years ago, I started shooting covers for romance authors in her honor."

Amara's eyes softened. "I'm so sorry for your loss."

He'd heard those words before, but coming from her, they felt....real.

"Thanks. She was my rock. I've got a good support system. They got me through it."

She picked up a copy from the top of the display and handed it to him. "Here you are." She glanced at the cover. "It's a beautiful shot."

"Thanks." His fingers brushed hers on the book. Neither of them moved right away.

"RYAAAAAN!" Mrs. Jones called from the counter.

"That must be your coffee," Amara said. "Congrats again on the cover."

"It's Ryan Hartwell, by the way." He extended his hand.

"Amara Jones. As in, daughter of Jones Café," she said, then winced. "Wow. I don't know why I said that."

He smiled as he walked away. Amara stayed back, catching her breath. Moments like that only happened in movies. She wanted to text the girls immediately, but for now she let herself savor it.

"Thanks for the coffee and the book, Mr. and Mrs. Jones!" Ryan called out. "Can't wait to try the crepe. Love supporting Black businesses."

The bell chimed behind him as he left.

"What a nice, handsome young man," Mrs. Jones said, wiping the counter.

"Yes, he was," Mr. Jones added, stepping out from the back. "Now that's the kind of man I want you to bring home, Mara."

"Alright, Dad, that's my cue." She grabbed her purse and keys. "Too late to talk about my love life." She hugged her parents. "Plus, don't you have a game to watch?"

She flipped the sign to CLOSED, locked the door and headed to her car, secretly wondering what it would be like to actually bring someone like Ryan home.

Chapter Three

"Why did you say your full name like an undercover spy or something?" Sadie snickered as she flipped through racks of dresses. They were hunting for something for Amara to wear to Kelsie's magazine cover launch. Having a celebrity stylist as a best friend came in handy at times like these.

Amara laughed as she turned a necklace over in her hand. "I kept thinking, 'What would Kelsie do?'"

"Pretty sure she wouldn't have done that." Sadie held a dress up to Amara, eyeing her like a tailor. "You know, I really should be charging you for my expertise."

Amara snatched the dress with a smirk and disappeared into the fitting room.

When she stepped out and saw herself in the mirror, she already knew. Committed. The dress hugged her hips, cinched her waist, and came in her favorite color palette.

"I should pay you," she admitted. "But you love me, so it's included in the friendship perks."

"What I'm hearing is, you love the dress and owe me lunch."

"Rain check. I have plans."

Sadie's eyes lit up. "Ooh! With Mr. Photographer? What's his name again? I thought nothing happened!"

"No. Not with 'Mr. Photographer'," she mocked. "And you don't need to know his name because nothing is going to happen." She nudged her. "I just need to shop for CeCe's loft."

It was technically true. Mostly. All she really needed to do was check in with her assistant Nina and finalize vendor selections. But lunch with Sadie meant Kelsie would join, which meant cocktails, which meant an accidental girls' night out. Tempting, but Amara wanted a cozy night alone.

"I still can't believe she picked me for this project," Amara said, grinning. "Thank you again for the connection."

"Friendship perks. Now before you go, shoes!"

They spent the next hour picking heels and accessories. Sadie teased her about Ryan the entire time, though her attention wandered the second a handsome stranger caught her eye. She flirted with him for ninety seconds before he asked her out.

"You're going with him tonight?" Amara asked, eyebrows raised.

"I invited him to meet me and Kelsie for drinks since someone rejected my invitation," Sadie sang. "Sure you don't want to come? It's Saturday. Work can wait."

"You two have fun. I really need to stay on schedule for CeCe."

They headed for the parking lot with their shopping bags.

"Be safe. And don't forget Sunday Dinner tomorrow," Amara called as she loaded her car.

"When have I ever missed Sunday Dinner at the Joneses?" Sadie replied, climbing into her vintage jade Bronco.

Amara pulled out first, already craving pajamas, fuzzy socks and her go-to blanket. She couldn't wait to sink into *Highway to Love*. She opened her food app and placed an order from Ronnie's. Bacon cheeseburger sliders with steak fries and a strawberry milkshake. A full burger would slow down her reading flow. And yes, she could listen to the audiobook, but turning actual pages was part of the magic.

Thirty minutes later she pulled into her driveway. Thank God for hands-free features. She waved her foot under the bumper to close the trunk, arms full with her bags, purse and most sacred of all, her food.

She set her takeout on the kitchen island, hung the dress in her closet and changed into her cozy clothes. As she grabbed her book her phone rang.

"Hey Mom. Hi Dad. I know I'm on speaker," she said.

"Hey Cupcake!"

"Hey Mara!"

Her parents chimed together.

"I was just calling to confirm Kelsie and Sadie will be at dinner tomorrow," her mom said.

"Yes, all three of us will be there." She paused. Something in her mom's tone tripped her Spidey Senses. "Mom. What's the real reason you're calling?"

"That is why I called! Scout's honor! I just want to make enough yams and plantains for Sadie. Tomorrow is Jamaican night, and you know how much she loves them. But..."

"Here it comes," Amara muttered.

"Since I have you on the phone... guess what happened today?" Her mom's voice rose with excitement.

Last time this happened, her mom had set her up with a church friend's son who spilled red wine on a white Balmain dress Kelsie loaned her.

"That sweet handsome boy Ryan left us a review on that Black-Owned Business site!"

"Aww. That was nice of him, Mom." Amara tried to sound even though she knew this wasn't the end of it.

"He mentioned you. I just sent you a screenshot."

Butterflies flickered in her stomach. "Mom, I don't—" Her phone buzzed.

She looked.

Between the chill vibes, the apple cinnamon crepes that took me straight back to my mom's kitchen, and the radiant barista who helped me find the book I needed, Jones Cafe might be my new favorite spot in the city.

Her heart stuttered. Then the cold from her milkshake hit her temple like punishment.

"Amara! Mara? You still there, honey?"

"I told you we would lose service going this way," her mom scolded in the background.

"She's probably still there. Cupcake?" her dad said.

"Yeah, I'm here. Brain freeze," she croaked.

"He's obviously smitten, Mara. Did you give him your number?"

"Mom!"

"I know, baby. I just want you to be happy."

"I appreciate that. But I've gotta go. Love you. See you tomorrow."

"We love you too!"

She hung up and stared down at her book. The butterflies now danced to the rhythm of her racing heart. Ryan had captured something real on this cover. The couple stood forehead to forehead, a soft heart-shaped space between them. Behind them, black pavement faded into a sunset of violets, oranges and golds.

It was breathtaking.

Beep! Beep!

Her food was warm. A perfect distraction from the dangerous path of Googling him, stalking his socials, and crafting entire romantic scenarios in her head. This was just a crush. A harmless flex of her flirting muscles. Nothing more.

She plated her sliders and fries on a bamboo tray, set her shake beside it and carried everything to the living room. Leaving her phone and the book jacket on the island. There would be no more distractions.

Wrapped in her blanket, she opened her book, took a bite of her slider and let herself fall into the world of Brandi Hicks.

This was the only romance she would allow in.

Chapter Four

The scent of jerk seasoning, thyme and scotch bonnet peppers drifted through the Jones home like a warm welcome.

"Come on, ref! Open your eyes!" her father shouted the moment Amara stepped inside.

"He was in the zone! That's a touchdown!" Sadie shrieked back from the couch.

When Mrs. Jones found out Sadie was in Georgia alone for college, she'd folded her right into Sunday dinners like a lost daughter. That quickly led to Sadie's chaotic love affair with football. Mr. Jones was thrilled to finally have someone who matched his game-day energy. Amara had tried being his football buddy, but she barely made it through one quarter without reaching for a book and a drink.

"Hey Sadie, hey Dad," Amara called, heading toward the kitchen.

Both of them waved without looking away from the TV.

"Hi!" Sadie chirped absently.

"MOM! Dad's hogging Sadie again!"

"Jerome! Stop stealing Amara's friends!" her mother yelled back, her Jamaican lilt slipping through.

Mrs. Jones swayed by the stove, humming reggae as she checked the jerk chicken.

"Knew you'd break out the accent tonight. Need help?" Amara teased, kissing her cheek.

"You can chop the lettuce."

"I can cook, you know. I live alone. I eat."

"You do, baby. It's just not... good." She patted her daughter's cheek, then slid a cutting board across the counter. "Chop and toss. Make it pretty. Everything's irie."

"Pretty sure that's not how 'irie' works, Mom."

"TOUCHDOWN!" her dad and Sadie hollered, drowning out the knock at the back door.

"It's open!" Mrs. Jones called.

Kelsie glided in like she was walking a runway, heels clicking, bakery box in hand.

"Mmm, smells delicious!" she sang, setting the box down. "Rum cake for dessert."

"Bless your heart," Mrs. Jones said. "And your shoes are cute too!"

"Why do you insist on wearing heels to Sunday dinner?" Amara asked, hugging her friend.

"Because some of us go into the church building."

"I receive the Word in my robe and slippers on the couch," Amara countered, popping a crouton in her mouth.

"Besides," Kelsie added, "you never know who you might run into. I might even let you borrow these heels for your next run-in with Mr. Photographer."

Sadie popped in the kitchen with a bowl of chips. "She told you about his review? Radiant barista?"

"Sadie!" Amara groaned. "I'm leaving. Kelsie, I'm getting you some socks."

She overheard Sadie asking about more guac as she walked away.

"No," Mrs. Jones said, snatching the bowl. "Dinner's almost ready. Call Jerome."

"Yes ma'am."

She vanished again.

Mrs. Jones turned to Kelsie. "Anything new with you? I heard you have a big event coming up."

"Yes ma'am," Kelsie said proudly. "A cover launch featuring the Stormriders starting five. All women. All power."

"I love that. About time they got the spotlight."

"And before anyone asks," Kelsie added, "Marcus is not invited. I don't care who he reps."

Amara entered, socks in hand. The mention of Marcus' name sucked the air out of the room.

"Well," Amara said gently, "can CeCe come? She's a fan of yours."

"I'd love that. I'm bringing someone too."

"A man," Mrs. Jones guessed.

"MOM!"

"It's fine," Kelsie said. "I'd tell Mama J anyway."

The women finished setting the table as soon as the game ended. All the guests gathered around the table, family style. The air was warm with spices, laughter and home.

"Okay," Mrs. Jones said between bites. "Y'all will be at Open Mic Night, right?"

"Absolutely," Sadie said.

"Just give me the date," Kelsie added. "I'll have my assistant block it."

"I don't think I have a choice," Amara joked.

Mr. Jones stood and stretched. "Dinner was amazing, ladies. I'm gonna check out some highlights."

He slipped away suspiciously fast.

Amara shot a look at the table. "Are those flash cards?"

"Quick! Block the door!" Kelsie yelled.

Mrs. Jones moved like a linebacker. Sadie threw an arm across Amara's chest.

"Amara," Sadie said, throwing the flash cards dramatically in the air, "tonight, we plan your birthday."

"Surprise!" her mom posed.

"Noooo," Amara groaned.

"Honey," Mrs. Jones said softly, "if you don't move forward, you'll stay stuck in that night forever. Let's celebrate you."

Over the next two hours, they debated themes, ate rum cake and laughed until their stomachs hurt. Mr. Jones returned to cast the deciding vote.

A nineties-inspired pajama party.

"Your birthday is on Saturday," Kelsie said. "Party then?"

"Let's do Friday," Amara said. "People might have actual Valentine's plans."

"Absolutely not," Sadie said. "We are not hosting your comeback party on Friday the 13th."

"How about Thursday?" Kelsie offered. "Grown and sexy, early night, leaves the weekend open."

"Fine," Amara said. "But I get veto power on outfits."

"Deal," Kelsie said. "Invites are ready. Want to press send?"

Amara hovered her mouse.

"I can't believe I'm doing this..."

Click.

The room erupted.

On her drive home with rum cake and leftovers beside her, a small smile curled her lips. For the first time in years, she was looking forward to her birthday.

Chapter Five

CeCe Hughes' home was the kind of place interior designers fantasized about. Spacious, sunlit and effortlessly styled. The loft alone had two-story windows, skylights, and exposed beams. It felt like a blank canvas begging for something beautiful.

Amara followed CeCe into the kitchen. Double islands gleamed under pendant lights. A walk-in pantry sat off to the side, and the chrome appliances looked like they belonged in a magazine.

Amara set her tote on the island and pulled out her tablet filled with mood boards and swatches.

"So," CeCe said, sipping kombucha from a tall glass, "what's your vision? I'm dying to know."

They moved into the loft corner, sun warming Amara's shoulders as she sketched. Their conversation bounced easily, more like two creatives vibing than a designer and client.

Hours later, the design lived on her tablet in full color. A neutral palette of sand, cream and soft terracotta. A linen sectional draped in raw silk and organic cotton pillows. A Moroccan rug layered beneath a low sculptural coffee table. Built-in bookshelves. Earth-tone abstract art. CeCe's family heirlooms repurposed into a custom coffee table book.

"You just get it," CeCe said. "Sadie was right."

Footsteps sounded from upstairs.

"Baby, I'm heading to the stadium," a baritone voice called.

CeCe didn't look up. "Don't forget to ice that shoulder!"

"Don't forget to kiss me."

Andre Hughes appeared, all broad shoulders and confidence, halfway out the door until he detoured to kiss CeCe's cheek and grab her curves with a grin.

"Stop, baby," CeCe giggled. "We have company."

Andre looked up at Amara, smiling. "You don't mind seeing Black love in action, do you?"

"Not at all," she laughed. "Grew up with it. My parents are worse."

He nodded. "Good to meet you, Amara."

When he left, CeCe turned back with mischief in her eyes.

"You two are ridiculous," Amara teased.

"That's my man my man my man," CeCe smirked. "So... are you dating anyone?"

"Nope."

"Lying."

"Atlanta is... Atlanta."

"Whew. Trust me, I know." CeCe leaned against the island. "I almost curved Dre when we met. He showed up to one of my events with a Pinterest board. Had the nerve to title it 'Our Dream Home.'"

Amara choked. "Tell me you blocked him."

"Almost. But something said wait. He showed up again. And again. Between the peonies and the playlist he made for me... I just knew he was my husband."

"Persistence," Amara murmured.

"The good kind."

Amara nodded but her mind drifted. Ryan's low Texan voice had been echoing in the back of her head all week.

"You okay?" CeCe asked.

"Yeah," Amara lied. "Just thinking."

When they finished packing up, Amara paused at the door.

"Kelsie would love for you to attend the cover launch Thursday night by the way."

"I'm there," CeCe said. "I'll bring the heels and the energy."

Chapter Six

CeCe touched up her makeup in the backseat of her Cadillac Escalade as she thanked Amara for inviting her to the magazine launch. They stepped out to flashing cameras and a chorus of photographers shouting CeCe's name. After a handful of poses they made their way inside.

Since the Atlanta Stormriders were on the cover, Kelsie had transformed the venue into an upscale sports bar. Stormrider purple and cream decorated the space. A champagne tower sat beside a basketball-shaped ice sculpture. Servers dressed as cheerleaders passed out "playbooks" that listed cocktails and appetizers, while the bartenders, dressed like referees, mixed themed drinks behind the bar.

Bar-height tables surrounded the space, and the dance floor stretched wide for the line dancing Kelsie insisted on adding to every celebration. Amara spotted her near a high-top, glowing in a purple designer dress that showed off her runway legs. Kelsie stayed media-ready without trying. They made their way over and Kelsie's smile instantly widened.

"I'm so glad you're here!" she squealed, pulling Amara into a hug.

She greeted CeCe next. "I was looking forward to meeting you tonight."

"I've been excited to meet you too," CeCe replied. They exchanged air kisses before linking arms.

"Let's grab a drink and head to VIP," Kelsie said. "Amara, you coming?"

"For a drink, yes," Amara said. "But y'all enjoy VIP. I see Sadie walking in."

Sadie entered with her usual rockstar aura. Slick low ponytail, a custom Sadie Goodman pantsuit in Stormrider purple and cream, and diamond-studded basketball cufflinks. She hugged everyone warmly and immediately began scanning the menu.

"I really hope there's shrimp in this playbook," she said.

"I didn't see shrimp," Amara replied, "but those parmesan-crusted crab-stuffed mushrooms? Elite."

Sadie pointed. "Flag down a cheerleader. I'm starving!"

Within minutes, the server returned with two plates of mushrooms... and just in time for their second glass of champagne.

Amara reached for a fresh flute and froze as a warm, steady forearm brushed against hers. A rough hand closed over the same glass. A quiet shiver ran up her spine.

"My bad," a deep voice said. "Here, you can have this one."

That voice sounded so familiar. She looked up.

Ryan.

They both held onto the flute, unwilling to let go.

Sadie whipped around.

"Amara! There are plenty of other glasses. Sorry about my friend. She's very territorial when it comes to her champagne apparently."

Ryan chuckled and released the flute, his smile slow and knowing.

Before Amara could recover, a voice floated over her shoulder.

"Hey, Ryan!"

Kelsie. But how did she know Ryan?

She strolled up, eyes narrowing when she clocked the vibe between the three of them.

"You two know each other?" she asked, looking between Amara and Ryan with investigative glee.

"I'm trying to figure that out myself." Sadie said, doing nothing to hide her amusement.

Kelsie's eyes widened as the dots connected.

"Wait... wait... HOLD ON."

She pointed at Ryan. "*Ryan* is Mr. Photographer?!"

He smirked, leaning closer to Amara. "So you have been talking about me."

She rolled her eyes and took a long sip almost emptying the glass.

Kelsie gasped, delighted. "Oh my God, Amara. We can double date!"

"Relax," Amara muttered.

Ryan greeted Kelsie properly. "Good to see you again, Kels."

"Thank you again for the Stormrider cover," she said. "You killed it."

"You know I had to show up for Malik's girl. You're family now." he replied.

Kelsie smirked. "Where is he anyway?"

Ryan pointed across the room.

"Over there."

They all followed his finger. Standing in the middle of a captivated crowd was a tall, golden-brown man with a beard, a curly taper, and a fitted shirt that had no business fitting that well. He was mid-story, hands flying as people laughed around him.

"MALIK CHAMPION!" Sadie blurted, nearly choking on a mushroom.

Kelsie smirked like she'd been waiting for the moment.

"You said he was a studio owner!"

"In her defense, he is," Ryan said. "After his injury he had more time on his hands and wanted to help me get my name out there. That's how 3Kings started."

Kelsie added, "Yes, had I known he was the same photographer you met at the café, Mar, I would've said something."

Before Amara could respond, Malik's slid into the group effortlessly, dapping Ryan up and pulling Kelsie in for a kiss on the cheek.

Sadie blinked. "Where's the third 'King'?"

Malik nodded toward the bar. "King. Over there."

They looked over to see a tall, golden-toned man with locs in a loose bun, glasses perched low on his nose. White button-down clinging to him like he was Clark Kent. He flirted with the bartender, drink in one hand, a napkin with a number in the other. Just as Amara prepared her exit strategy, Malik dropped another bomb.

"By the way, Kels — Ryan agreed to do your friend's birthday shoot."

Amara froze. "Wait... *he* is taking my pictures?"

Ryan didn't miss a beat. "I take more than just book cover photos, you know."

Before she could form a comeback, King strutted over.

"Good evening," he said, dapping Malik and Ryan, then turning to Sadie with a grin. "King Williams. And you are?"

Sadie gave him a once-over and laughed. "You wish."

"I'm heading to VIP," she announced to her friends. "Can't let this suit go to waste."

"You don't have to worry about that," King called after her. "Whatever you were trying to do? Mission accomplished."

She rolled her eyes and strutted away. King followed like a man who'd found his next challenge.

Malik shook his head. "That's my cue."

"And mine," Kelsie added. "Sadie may be tiny, but she'll go full ninja if needed."

They headed off, leaving Amara alone with Ryan — exactly what she didn't want.

"Will it be a problem?" Ryan asked softly.

"What?"

"Me taking your birthday pictures."

"That depends," she said.

He lifted a brow.

"How're you liking *Highway to Love*?"

He looked down at his champagne. "I haven't read it. I take the photos, buy the books... but reading them? I don't do that."

She gasped dramatically. "Absolutely not. Read the first three chapters and then I'll think about letting you take my pictures."

He stepped closer, breath brushing her cheek.

"A private book club, huh?" His gaze dipped to her lips. "Set the time and place... I'm there."

He stepped back, biting his bottom lip just enough for her to notice.

Before the moment could tilt too far, CeCe appeared.

"The driver is here. Unless," she followed Amara's gaze. "you've already got a ride?"

Amara tore her eyes from Ryan. "No. I'm ready."

She turned to him. "Nice seeing you again."

"Likewise," he said. "I'll see you next week."

"Only if you finish those three chapters."

She took CeCe's hand and walked away, but not without glancing back one more time.

Chapter Seven

Ryan adjusted the lighting setup at the studio, mentally checking everything one last time. It had been in place for hours, but he couldn't sit still. His phone buzzed again. The chat had been blowing up all morning.

Malik: Don't fuck this up, bro. She's Kelsie's girl.

King: But if you do. I don't mind picking up the slack. She fine as hell.

Ryan silenced the group chat. Kelsie had asked for a favor and he'd said yes, not knowing the "friend" she needed him to shoot was Amara. He'd been annoyed at himself for weeks for walking out of the café without her number, talking himself out of showing up there again like some lovesick teenager.

But fate handled it for him.

The second he got home that night he grabbed *Highway to Love* off his shelf. He meant to skim a few pages so he could say he'd started it, but once he opened it he didn't stop.

The main character, Riley, was guarded. Tough on the outside, shut down on the inside. He knew that type of hurt. He knew what it looked like to let people close enough to enjoy you but not close enough to know you. He'd been doing that for years without calling it what it was.

When his mom passed he learned how to keep things light. Be the guy who made people laugh, kept things easy, never going deeper than the surface. With women it was even simpler. Chemistry, sex, a vibe for the night. Nothing real. Nothing that required him to open the parts of himself he'd boarded up.

It kept things safe. But Amara unlocked something in him that night at the cafe and now, he was knee deep in a romance novel he'd originally bought just as a memento.

His nerves were getting loud so he picked up his camera and fired off a test shot just to steady himself. Then the soft click of the studio door opened.

He heard the soft click of the studio door. Amara stepped inside, casual and cozy, curls tucked under a satin scarf, makeup already flawless. There was nothing dramatic about her entrance. She didn't try to command the room. But damn if she didn't.

"Hey," she said softly.

"Hey." His voice sounded deeper than usual. He cleared his throat. "You made it."

She smiled. "Yeah. Hard to miss the giant crowns in the parking lot."

He tried not to stare. Failed. "King's idea," he said, rubbing the back of his neck as heat crept beneath his shirt.

"Where do I get ready?" she asked, glancing around.

"Come on," he said. "I'll show you."

He walked her down the hallway, aware of how close she was to him. He could feel her eyes on him. He could feel everything, but he needed to look unaffected.

"Kelsie had me set something up for you in there," he said. His hand brushed the doorframe, brushing closer to her than he meant to. "Come back when you're ready."

She stepped inside and the door clicked shut, leaving him alone in the hallway.

His jaw tightened as heat crawled up his neck. He forced himself to focus on the lights, the camera, the damn floor, anything but how good she looked. Because all he could picture was her curls freed from that scarf, tumbling around her face with every slow rise and fall of her body.

He dragged in a breath, sharp and punishing. Get it together, man. This is a job. Just take the damn pictures. The soft, steady click of heels drifted down the hall shook him out of his fantasy. And every thought he wasn't supposed to have came rushing back.

Chapter Eight

Amara pulled into the parking lot of 3Kings Studio and sat in the car with her hair set in rods beneath a satin scarf, makeup already done, oversized jogger set and Ugg slippers in place.

"Sadie, why won't you just tell me what's in the bag?" she asked through Bluetooth, staring at the garment bag on the passenger seat like it was plotting against her.

"Because if I told you, you would've punked out. Too late now, boo."

"I truly hate you sometimes."

"Put all that energy into the shoot, ma'am. Mr. Photographer's fine ass is waiting for you."

"That is not helping." Her cheeks burned. "Let me get out of this car before I change my mind. Talk later."

"Don't do anything I wouldn't do!"

Amara cut the engine and headed inside. The studio door carried the 3Kings crown logo, and the moment she stepped through it she was wrapped in the familiar scent of bergamot and sandalwood, an intoxicating mix she now associated with Ryan.

The space was dimly lit. Black-and-white portraits covered the walls with a bold hand-painted mural of Ryan, Malik and King in the center. Each of their heads formed the points of the crown. Neo-soul drifted through the air, steady and grounding.

She followed the light to the set where Ryan adjusted his camera. He wore a gray beanie and a white T-shirt that clung to his chest and arms. Her eyes wandered down to his gray sweatpants and she mentally slapped herself.

"You made it," Ryan said, smiling.

"Yeah, kinda hard to miss the giant crowns on the parking lot signs."

"King's idea," he said, dimples peeking beneath his beauty mark. They locked eyes, and something warm stretched between them. She looked away first.

"Where do I get ready?"

He scratched the back of his neck, muscles shifting beneath his shirt. Heat rolled through her so fast she mentally pinched herself. *Girl, behave.*

"Come on," he said. "I'll show you."

She followed him down the hallway, her eyes casually roaming over his athletic build. He stopped at a sleek black door with a gold logo.

"Kelsie had me set something up for you in there," he said. "Come back when you're ready."

Inside the dressing room, Amara found a small spread. Chilled champagne, a glass, chocolate-covered strawberries, vanilla-scented body oil and a handwritten note from Kelsie telling her to relax.

"Of course she did," Amara muttered, grinning.

She poured champagne and took a long sip. Oh God, this is actually happening. Finally she unzipped the garment bag.

"Oh, hell no."

A brown satin nightgown dress with a matching robe. Nude stilettos. So that's why Sadie insisted on pedicures.

She finished her champagne and poured another. After a pep talk in the mirror she stepped into the dress, slipped on the heels and unraveled her curls. Her hair bounced around her shoulders like a halo. She fluffed it, touched up her lipstick and stepped back.

Damn.

Whether it was the champagne or the glow-up she looked incredible. She tied her robe loosely and headed back to the set.

♥

Ryan turned at the sound of her heels. His eyes tracked her every step, taking in the way the satin hugged her hips and thighs, the soft bounce of her curls, the robe trailing behind her like a slow-motion fantasy.

"You're lucky," she said lightly.

"Lucky?"

"I really shouldn't be here," she teased. "You never read the first three chapters, remember?"

Ryan stepped closer, eyes locked on hers. "And what makes you think I didn't?"

"Well did you?"

"I can relate to Riley," he said, adjusting his lens. "Losing someone like that. Guarding your heart after. I've been there."

Her heart softened. She reached for his arm, gave it a gentle squeeze. "I'm sorry, Ryan."

He shrugged. "I promised I'd read it. I'm halfway through."

Her brows lifted. "Halfway? Wow. Look at you becoming a whole Hickie."

They laughed, the sound softening into something warmer. She realized her hand still on his arm like it belonged there, and quickly pulled it back.

"So," she cleared her throat. "Where do you want me?"

Her voice came out lower than she intended. Champagne was definitely hitting.

"Right here," he said, pointing. And his accent? Deeper. Rougher. Her body responded before she could stop it.

She stepped onto the marked spot. "Uhm... I've never modeled before. Am I just... smiling? Holding a pillow? What's the vibe?"

"Just be yourself. Have fun. Forget I'm even here."

Easy for him to say.

Ryan sensed her nerves and handed her a satin pillow. "Here. Start with this."

Soon she loosened up, remembering Kelsie's note. She played with her hair, twirled her robe, laughed as she moved with the music.

"Let's try something else," Ryan said. "Do you trust me?"

She nodded, slow but certain.

He led her to a corner of the studio where pillows and soft sheets were spread across the floor, the lighting warm and dim. "Sit here. Lean back. Let your robe fall a little."

She followed his cue, the robe slipping from her shoulder. Ryan stepped in to adjust her strap, his fingers skimming her skin with a touch that stole her breath.

Her mind ran ahead of her, imagining those fingers trailing lower. Before she could stop herself she leaned in and kissed him. A soft, tentative press.

Ryan jolted back, surprised.

"I—I'm sorry," Amara whispered. She stood quickly, gathering her things. "I shouldn't have. I've never—"

He caught her wrist gently and pulled her back toward him. His hand rose to her cheek, thumb brushing her skin as he leaned in.

"You have no idea what you do to me," he said, voice deep and rough.

He kissed her, firm, sure.

Her fingers slid into his beard, something she'd wanted since the café. He groaned as she tugged at the hem of his shirt. He stripped it off in one smooth motion.

"Wait," she said breathlessly, "I want to see you."

He leaned back, letting her take him in. His chest, abs, that wicked V disappearing below his waistband, the fraternity brand above his heart.

"You ready?" he asked.

She bit her lip, letting her robe fall. "I'm ready for you, Ryan."

He lifted her leg and lowered her into the pillows. He removed her heels with slow kisses along her ankle and up her leg. His hands spread across her thighs, warm and reverent.

"God, you're thick," he murmured before biting into her inner thigh. A moan escaped her.

Her thong disappeared in his hand. His mouth followed, trailing kisses, licks and gentle bites up her thighs until he reached her center.

"Ryan... please," she gasped.

"Tell me what you want."

"Higher," she begged.

He obeyed.

Her whole body arched as he tasted her. He feasted with care and hunger, pulling every ounce of pleasure from her until she tightened around him, thighs clenching. She gripped the sheets, pillows, his shoulders, whatever she could hold onto as pleasure rolled through her.

A cry broke free from her throat. "Oh my Goooood, Ryan!"

He kissed up her body, lingering at the rose tattoo on her hip. He slid her dress over her head, unhooked her bra and whispered against her skin, "You're so damn sexy."

"I'd say the same but I'm the only one naked."

"You're right."

His pants hit the floor, black briefs barely containing him.

"Come here," she moaned.

Their mouths crashed together as he reached for a condom. His thumb circled her sensitive center until she came again, thighs trembling.

He pushed into her, slowly, deeply, taking her breath away. They moved like they already knew each other. Her legs wrapped around his waist as he lifted her, worshipping her with every thrust.

He knelt with her cradled in his arms, rocking her up and down until she tightened again and they both came undone, their cries echoing off the studio walls. He collapsed back, pulling her onto his chest. Her breaths matched his. Wrapped in each other, bodies humming and hearts thundering, they drifted to sleep tangled in satin and sheets.

Chapter Nine

She rolled over and blinked at an unfamiliar ceiling. For a second she didn't move, suspended between sleep and reality. Then it hit her.

Satin pillows.

Champagne.

Ryan's mouth on her skin.

"Shit."

She bolted upright so fast the blanket slipped down her chest. Heat rushed to her face as she scrambled off the studio floor, grabbing her heels and sweeping her clothes into her arms like she was escaping a crime scene.

She tiptoed to the dressing room and closed the door behind her, pressing her back against it as her pulse hammered in her ears. Her phone sat on the vanity beside the half-empty bottle of champagne.

6:30 p.m.

"Shit, shit, shit!"

She yanked on her joggers backwards, didn't bother fixing them, and stuffed everything into her bag with shaky hands. This wasn't her. Amara didn't do impulsive! She definitely didn't do studio hookups with men she barely knew. Except... apparently, she did.

She tried to shove down the flashbacks. His hands on her thighs, her own voice moaning his name like she'd been waiting years to say it like that. She had to escape! Swiftly, but quietly.

She slipped out the front door and sprinted barefoot across the parking lot. She jumped into her SUV, turned the ignition, and backed out only for her rear sensors to explode with warning beeps.

She slammed the brakes.

Ryan stood behind her car.

Shirtless.

Sweatpants hanging low on his hips.

Chest still flushed from everything they had done.

His eyes locked with hers.

She mouthed, *Sorry*, then threw the car into drive and peeled out like she was outrunning the FBI. She didn't stop until she reached a nearby Ulta. Still barefoot, she hissed at her phone, "Hey Siri, FaceTime Girls with the Tattoos."

Sadie popped up first, eyes widening. "Amara Maaaaar—ohhh. It was like that?"

"Do not start," Amara warned.

"I'm just saying, you look freshly... exercised."

Kelsie joined the call mid-sentence. "Okay, y'all have five minutes—" She froze. Took one look at Amara. Snapped her fingers. "Sara? Push that call to tomorrow. We have a crisis."

She settled in with a bowl of grapes. "Talk. Now."

"You hussies," Amara muttered.

"We love you too," Sadie said sweet as syrup.

Amara pointed at her screen. "You! Sadie. Lingerie? Heels? Really?"

"I thought it'd be sultry for the birthday. Clearly it worked." Sadie shrugged.

"And you!" She swung to Kelsie. "Champagne. Strawberries. Body oil. Y'all set me up!"

Kelsie grinned. "I see your curls are still doing the walk of shame. You're welcome."

"When are you going to tell us what happened with Mr. Photographer?" Sadie asked.

"I'm not telling y'all nothing."

They gasped like a Greek chorus. Sadie waved a white cloth dramatically.

"Okay! We yield!"

"Fine. But only if we debrief in person. Sadie, dinner on you. Kels, I left the strawberries and champagne behind in the chaos. Please tell me you're handling it."

"Already on my way," Kelsie said. "But this sounds like tequila, not champagne."

"Agreed," Amara said. "Fajitas and margaritas. I need the carbs."

Her friends exchanged a mischievous glance.

"I saw that!"

"Carbs," Sadie said confidently. "I'm ordering from Prima's now."

An hour later, Amara was home with music humming through her speakers. She removed her makeup and reached for the toner when she spotted it in the mirror.

A bright red mark blooming on her neck.

She groaned. "You've got to be kidding me."

She pressed a cold compress against it and accepted her fate.

After a long shower she slipped into her coziest pajamas, tied her hair up in a bonnet, and slid into her slippers. The doorbell rang just as she finished.

Her camera feed lit up.

Kelsie and Sadie stood on the porch, grinning like devils, margarita mix and takeout in hand.

Let the interrogation begin.

Chapter Ten

"C'mon, girl, it's cold out here!" Kelsie barked into Amara's Ring camera, glaring like the device had personally offended her.

"And I am starving—both for the food and the tea," Sadie added, yanking her coat tighter.

Amara laughed and unlocked the door. "You two are so dramatic. It hasn't even been two minutes."

"Two minutes too long," Sadie said, breezing past her. "The fajitas are seconds from tragedy."

She dropped the takeout bags on the kitchen island and immediately started unpacking foil trays. Amara grabbed plates while Kelsie drifted to the bar cart, humming as she mixed margaritas. Within moments, they were all seated with full plates and chilled drinks.

Kelsie pointed her margarita at Amara. "Alright. You've got carbs, you've got tequila. Spill. What happened at the shoot?"

Amara took the world's slowest bite of fajita, chased it with an even slower sip of margarita, then finally surrendered and told them everything.

Every look.

Every touch.

Every whispered name.

Every moment she absolutely should have left... and every moment she chose to stay.

"And then I called you guys," she finished, cheeks warm.

Silence.

Kelsie clutched her diamond pendant like a prayer. Sadie froze mid-bite, her fajita suspended in midair.

"I passed out on his chest," Amara added quietly. "Like... passed out passed out."

Kelsie shot up straight. "DAAAAAAAMN, girl! AND YOU JUST LEFT?"

Sadie stood to clap. "And don't forget the part where he ran out after her! Shirtless....into the parking lot! And she still peeled off like Fast & Furious: Heartbreak Drift!"

Kelsie tapped the island. "You better lock that man down."

"He is not my man!"

Sadie raised a brow. "Well... if he isn't... can he be mine?"

A tortilla chip flew at her face.

"Kidding! Kidding!" Sadie ducked. "But for real, Mara, why not?"

"Why not what?"

Kelsie leaned in, voice gentler. "Why not give Mr. Photographer a real chance? The chemistry is ridiculous. That kind of heat doesn't just happen."

"I'm not looking for anything serious right now," Amara muttered, a little more defensive than she meant to be.

Sadie groaned and slapped the counter. "Oh my God, Amara. That's such a cop-out. Nobody goes LOOKING for love. That's literally the point. It shows up when you aren't checking for it."

"Love is a strong word. We literally just had sex."

But even as she said it, something fluttered in her chest. "This isn't a romcom," she added. "Real life doesn't work like, 'Hey, I helped you find a book at a café and now we're in love.'"

Kelsie tilted her head. "What if he wants more?"

"He doesn't."

"How do you know?"

Amara couldn't answer. Her breath hitched, just barely, and her friends caught it.

"Can we not do this?" she said softly. "Can we just... change the subject?"

Sadie took the cue and stuffed the rest of her fajita in her mouth. Kelsie silently refilled Amara's margarita to the brim.

"Thank you," Amara sighed.

"One more thing," Sadie said, unable to resist.

Amara groaned. "What now?"

Sadie lifted a finger. "Hear me out. He photographed your favorite author's new book. Your parents adore him—"

"My parents adore everyone."

"Shhh!" Kelsie clapped a hand over her mouth. "Let her cook."

Sadie continued, eyes sparkling. "He vibed with your parents; he's best friends with Kelsie's—"

"Ex," Kelsie corrected. Instantly, both women whipped their heads toward her.

Kelsie waved her hand. "My chaos later. Amara's now. Continue."

Sadie blinked. "Has it been three months already?"

"Sadie," Amara warned, fighting a smile.

"Okay! All I'm saying is, every connection between y'all? Every little coincidence? That's fate doing backflips. You might want this to be casual, but it does not feel casual."

Amara reached across the island and squeezed her hand. "Thank you for your TED Talk, Dr. Goodman. But it's still a no."

Sadie threw her head back. "Amaraaaaa!"

"Sadie Marie Goodman!"

"Why'd you hit me with my government name!?" Sadie yelped, and the room dissolved into laughter.

As the giggles faded, Amara wiped her eyes. "Your turn, Kels."

Kelsie stood, lifted her glass, then marched toward the bar cart.

"We're gonna need more tequila."

Chapter Eleven

Ryan was still shirtless, barefoot, and pacing the studio like he'd misplaced his sanity somewhere between the dressing room and the bedroom setup. The vanity lights were dimmed now, casting a warm golden wash over the half-empty champagne bottle and the untouched chocolate-covered strawberries.

Everything was exactly where Amara left it.

Except her.

He picked up the robe she'd forgotten on the couch, fingers brushing the silky fabric, then set it gently on his chair. For a moment he stood still, staring at nothing, wondering how the day had gone from fire to fallout in minutes.

The door opened.

"Damn," King said, stepping inside with a protein shake. "Why it smell like love, lust and sin in here?"

"Sex and regrets," Malik added as he followed him in. "Heavy on the sex."

Ryan didn't look up. "Y'all ever heard of knocking?"

"This ain't the Four Seasons man," King said. "It's 3Kings. We own this place, remember?"

Malik scanned the room. The scattered pillows. The robe. The champagne. The fact that Ryan looked like he'd gone twelve rounds with his own emotions.

"Wait," Malik said slowly. "This from that shoot?"

Ryan nodded.

King let out a low whistle. "Whew."

Ryan dragged a hand over his face. "It wasn't supposed to happen like this."

Malik crossed his arms. "So that's why she flew outta here like her car was on fire. She nearly ran me over in the lot. Girl looked spooked. What happened? Besides the obvious."

"She woke up and bolted," Ryan admitted. "Didn't even wait for me to say goodbye. I tried to stop her but she still left. Looked me dead in the mirror and hit the gas."

Malik groaned. "Great. Kels already mad at me. Now her best friend running out on you? I'm catching hell either way."

Ryan let out a humorless laugh. "Solidarity in suffering."

Malik clapped his shoulder. "Look. Maybe this is how I get back in good with Kels. Let me help you get your girl back."

Ryan shot him a look. "She's not my girl."

"Yet," Malik said. "But you're not acting like a man who's ready to let her walk."

King raised his shake. "Facts. And while we on the subject..." He lowered his voice. "Either of y'all seen Sadie lately? The way she was looking at the launch party? I need that. ASAP."

Ryan actually laughed. "You trying to shoot your shot at Sadie?"

"I'm just saying," King grinned. "If we fixing relationships tonight, I want in. We get your girl back, get Malik out the doghouse, and if Sadie just so happens to need a tall, fine, emotionally available man... I'm there."

Malik pointed at him. "Only if it means you're helping us fix this mess."

King nodded but his eyes were on his phone. "I'm in."

Ryan sat at his desk and pulled up the final shot from the shoot. The image hit him like a punch. Her soft mouth. Her eyes. The trust she'd given him before everything spiraled.

"So we're clear," Ryan said. "I'm not chasing her. I'm just not ready to give up."

King snorted. "Bro... judging from this video, you absolutely chased her."

"Video?" Ryan frowned.

King replayed the footage. The exterior camera caught it perfectly. Ryan sprinting shirtless after Amara's car like a man with zero self-preservation.

Malik started coughing from laughing. King had to hold onto the counter.

"It gets better every watch," King wheezed.

Ryan shook his head. "C'mon bruh, I'm already suffering enough."

"Fair," Malik said, wiping his eyes. "So what's the plan?"

Ryan clicked save on the image then stood and faced King.

"I've got an idea. And doesn't Rod still owe you a favor?"

King's grin stretched slow and dangerous.

"Oh yeah," he said. "He owes me big."

Chapter Twelve

Sadie: Meet me at my studio around 11.
I have a client needing a designer for
a baby's room! We can go to lunch from
here.

Sadie's text hit early that morning, and honestly, Amara didn't need convincing.

She replied that she was on the way, grabbed her portfolio with photos from three of her favorite nursery projects, and got moving. She needed the distraction. Birthday planning and follow-up emails couldn't drown out the flashbacks from the afternoon she'd spent on the studio floor at 3Kings. A new project would.

The CeCe install was nearly wrapped, Nina was finalizing the last delivery, and the caterer had confirmed the menu for her birthday party. Work was steady, life was moving, and now she needed to look the part.

She chose a rich brown pantsuit, a cream silk blouse, and nude heels that said professional but still fun. By the time she reached Sadie's studio, she finally felt like herself again.

"Good morning, Ms. Jones!" a bright voice called as she stepped inside.

"Good morning, Cheyenne," Amara smiled. "And please call me Amara. Ms. Jones makes me feel like I'm about to hand out detentions."

Cheyenne giggled behind oversized glasses. "Yes, Ms. Jon—Amara."

"Better. Is Sadie around? She's introducing me to a client."

"She's in the Spirit Room. Said her client came in with heavy energy and needed cleansing first."

Amara snorted. "Sounds about right."

Sadie's studio was split between fashion, glam, and full-on energy work. She refused to style anyone whose aura was "crunchy," because in her words, bad energy throws off the fit.

"Want me to walk you back?" Cheyenne offered.

"I'm good. But I will be requesting a raise for you while I'm in there."

Cheyenne cackled as Amara headed down the hallway. Right as she reached the Spirit Room, the door swung open and out stepped Sadie—and a woman Amara recognized instantly.

"Amara!" Sadie beamed, hugging her. "Perfect timing. I want you to meet Cleopatra Jackson."

Amara blinked. "Wow. Cleopatra, this is an honor. Your last album got me through some things."

The singer smiled, her smooth East London accent warm. "Thank you, love. Always good meeting a real fan."

"And congratulations on the baby. When's your due date?"

"January," Cleopatra said, resting a hand on her belly. "But we haven't announced the gender yet, so keep it quiet."

"Of course. All my clients sign mutual NDAs."

"Well, if you're anything like Sadie, I imagine I'll be hiring you."

Sadie clapped her hands. "Alright ladies, to my office."

The next hour flew by. Cleopatra was thoughtful and warm, with a softness that contrasted her powerhouse stage persona. She wanted the nursery to feel calm but regal, something fit for a little prince. Amara shared her work, listened carefully, and offered ideas that made Cleopatra's entire face light up. By the end, Nina was already drafting the NDA and invoice.

"It was lovely meeting you," Amara said, packing her tablet. "Are you joining us for lunch?"

Sadie shook her head. "Actually, Cleo and I are gonna stay. We're pulling options for her gender reveal. Cheyenne ordered food."

"Got it. I'll grab something to go and start sketching."

"Don't be boring," Sadie warned. "And Kelsie will still be there."

"Right. I'll text her."

Amara: Sadie can't make lunch but I'm still coming.

Five minutes into the drive, her phone rang.

"I'm almost there, Kels," she answered.

"Hey AJ," Kelsie sniffled.

"You sound awful. You want soup? Tea?"

"No, I just saw your message. I think I should stay home today." She coughed weakly.

"It's okay. I'll grab something quick and head out."

"No!" Kelsie blurted, voice jumping an octave. "I mean... excuse me." She sneezed. "You should sit down, have a drink, relax. Don't let our flaky asses ruin your lunch. You look forward to this, remember?"

"...are you sure you're okay?"

"I'm fine. Just resting. Bye!"

The sudden hang-up was suspicious. Add Sadie scheduling a client last minute and bailing? Something was off. She pulled into valet, stepped out of her car, and the truth smacked her straight in the face.

There he was.

Ryan.

Sitting alone on the patio, broad shoulders filling out a black tee, sunlight catching the curve of his jaw as he checked his phone.

Amara didn't breathe for a full two seconds.

Then she opened the Girls with the Tattoos chat.

```
Amara: I hate you guys. Cleopatra
distraction? Pretending to be sick?
You deserve an Oscar.
```

Sadie and Kelsie responded immediately with halo emojis.

They had set her up.

Again.

Chapter Thirteen

Amara flipped open her compact, touched up her hair and makeup, then channeled her best Olivia Pope strut as she headed toward the problem she was absolutely not ready for.

Ryan. Fine Ass. Hartwell.

All black everything, fresh line-up, calm intensity in his eyes. Her heart skipped like it forgot the assignment.

"Hi Ryan. I apologize for my friends. I'm sorry they dragged you out here."

"I don't know what you're talking about. I live a few blocks away. I come here for lunch all the time."

She rolled her eyes. "It's okay, you don't have to pretend. I already texted my so-called friends when I saw you. The jig is up."

"Ah, man. They could've at least given me a heads-up." He rubbed the back of his neck, amused. "But to be fair, it was a group effort. Malik and King helped too. You left so fast the other day I didn't get a chance to—"

"We don't need to talk about that," she hushed, glancing around. "Especially not here."

He reached for her hand and her knees nearly buckled from the flashback that instantly entered her mind.

"Look," he said softly, "we're already here. Let's have lunch. My treat. And I brought your proofs from the shoot. We'll call it a business meeting."

She swallowed, gaining composure. "You're lucky I'm starving."

She brushed past him toward the door. He caught up instantly, pulling it open for her.

"What? I can't be a gentleman at work?"

She shot him a look but stepped inside.

"Welcome back Mr. Hartwell," the hostess said, straightening like she'd just seen Idris Elba.

"Thank you. My second guest is here."

"Yes sir. Right this way."

They followed her upstairs where a soft guitar drifted through the air. This level was calm and intimate. The opposite of where she and the girls usually sat.

The hostess led them to a corner booth tucked behind an oversized plant wall. Cozy, warm lighting, a perfect view of the room.

"Thank you," Ryan said.

"You're welcome." The hostess blushed, her gaze dragging a little too long over him. Amara felt her jaw tighten in a way she did not appreciate.

"Your waiter will be with you shortly," the hostess added, slipping away.

Amara exhaled. "Once again, sorry for my friends."

"Why?" he asked, flipping open his menu.

"They clearly meant for this to be a date. Reserving this table? A little over the top."

He closed his menu, meeting her eyes. "Actually, I reserved the table."

She blinked. "Excuse me?"

"King knows the owner. It's the best seat in the house." He smiled. "Would've been lonely up here if you turned down this business meeting."

She rolled her eyes.

His gaze dropped, then lifted again. Her breath caught.

"Plus," he added casually, sitting back, "I knew you'd want to see what we created."

She blinked fast.

"The pictures." His grin was sinful.

Their waiter appeared. Tad! Of course it was Tad.

"Oh hey! It's just you today? Where's the gang?" he asked.

"Yup, just me," she said, smiling. "And my guest. This is Ryan."

"Nice to meet you, Tad," Ryan said. "What's popular today?"

She watched the whole exchange. The man could charm an ATM if he wanted. Even ordering lunch was sexy.

"I'll take a Caesar salad. And a Cosmo," she said when Tad turned to her.

"And the cheese sticks?" Tad asked knowingly.

She sighed. Yeah, they were here way too often.

"Yes please."

As Tad walked away, she crossed her arms. "Alright, Mr. Photographer. Proofs?"

"Yup. I can text the link now."

Her eyes narrowed. "Is that your way of asking for my number?"

His mouth curved. "Do you want me to ask for your number?"

She smirked. "You can send it to amaralove@amaradesigns.com."

He laughed. "So you really gonna make me work for it."

"Absolutely."

"You should have the link now," he said.

She opened the email. "Wow. These are beautiful. Is this even me?"

"Malik barely had to edit anything. That's all you."

She blushed. Hard. "Thanks."

"It's the truth."

She needed to redirect the conversation before she melted into the booth. "Explain 3Kings. Were y'all supposed to be an R&B group or something?"

He chuckled. "Give us more credit than that. All our names mean king."

"King is obvious, but Ryan and Malik do too?"

"Yup. My sister Rhiannon helped name the studio."

"You have a sister?"

"I do. I'm the oldest. You?"

"Nope. It's just me. I wanted siblings but God gave me Kelsie and Sadie."

"I get that. That's how Malik and King are for me."

"How'd you get into photography?"

"My mom. She gave me a Polaroid for my eighth birthday." His voice softened. "I remember her last day with us. She wore this crooked scarf my sister made. We did a little photoshoot. That day felt light somehow. It didn't feel like she was sick. The picture we took ended up being our Christmas card."

She touched his arm gently. "She sounds amazing."

"She was." He cleared his throat. "Sorry, that got deep for a first date."

She smiled. "Business meeting, you mean."

He smirked. "Sure. Will there be a second one?"

"Let's eat first, and see what happens."

They talked until plates were empty, then full again, then empty again. They shared stories, laughter, and confessions. A cold draft hit her.

Ryan noticed instantly. "You cold?"

"A little."

"We could leave. Or..." he stood, shrugged off his jacket without hesitation, and draped it around her shoulders. Then he slid beside her in the booth. "I could sit here and keep you warm, get another drink, and finish these cheese sticks." He lifted one. "There's no way these are vegan."

She laughed softly. "I know right!?"

"So, what do you say to my proposal?"

"Let's do it."

They ordered another round. Tad brought fresh cheese sticks on the house, and a new guitarist started playing. They were still talking like no time had passed at all. Her alarm buzzed, interrupting the world they created. "Ryan... it's 8:30." She held up her phone. "We've been here all day."

"Let me see." He grabbed her phone and squinted dramatically. "I can't see without my glasses."

She groaned. "You don't wear glasses."

"You don't know that." He tapped their phones together. "Now we have each other's numbers."

"Really? Pretending to have bad eyesight? That's new."

"It worked though." He grinned. "Come on. I'll walk you to valet."

Outside, she handed him his jacket back as her car pulled up.

"So, my sister, Rhiannon," he said, "there's an art exhibit Friday night. I'd love for you to come."

She hesitated. "Today was amazing. I really needed the break, but—"

"Bring your friends," he said gently. "We'll call it another business meeting."

She smiled. "If they're free, I'd love to come."

He brightened. "Text me. I'm the new contact in your phone."

She shook her head. "Bye, Ryan Hartwell."

"See you soon, Amara Jones."

Chapter Fourteen

"I can't believe you have us chaperoning your date with Mr. Photographer tonight," Kelsie protested, taking a slow drag from a tightly rolled joint before passing it to Amara.

All three women were gathered to get ready for Rhiannon's art exhibit. The moment Amara mentioned Ryan's invite, her friends agreed to come without hesitation. Sadie and Kelsie arrived early to help her pick an outfit, calm her nerves, and admire her charcuterie board skills before they got dressed themselves.

"You are not chaperoning anything."

"Oh, so it is a date," Sadie teased from the couch, reaching for the joint to keep it moving.

"It's not. We're just supporting a friend and his sister's event."

"Wow. He upgraded from a fling to a friend," Kelsie smirked.

"See?" Amara pointed between them, grabbing a piece of cheese and pepperoni. "This is why I don't tell y'all anything."

"Oh my God, just admit you like him, Mara."

"Right," Sadie agreed, rolling a cheese cube between her fingers before popping it in her mouth. "It's okay to like someone."

"And it's way past time for you to open that heart up again," Kelsie added. "Everyone isn't going to hurt you like that demon did. You gotta give people a chance."

Amara sighed, placing the joint in the ashtray and lighting an incense stick. "I'm not sure about Ryan yet."

Her friends groaned in unison.

"Since you won't admit the obvious," Sadie switched gears, "what else you got to eat? I've got the munchies and this coochie coo board isn't cutting it."

Laughter cracked the tension that filled the room.

Amara got up, stretched, and shoved a frozen pizza into the oven. Meanwhile, Kelsie wandered to her media station, flipping through vinyls. She pulled out an album to wind down with and another to turn them back up later.

Sadie and Amara mimicked Kelsie's giggles when she suddenly became distracted by her phone lighting up.

"New victim?" Sadie asked.

Kelsie rolled her eyes but couldn't hide her smile. "Malik is hardly a victim."

"MALIIIIK?" both women gasped in unison.

"Apparently he's going to be there tonight too."

"Oh God." Sadie fell dramatically across the couch. "That means King will be there."

"Be nice. You might end up liking him," Amara teased.

"Like how you like Ryan?" Sadie shot back, sending Kelsie into a laughing fit.

Amara rolled her eyes, fighting the smile tugging at her mouth.

"Mhmm. Just like it. Come on, let's find your outfit for your date," Sadie sang, snatching her drink and sprinting toward Amara's bedroom.

"I'LL BE IN YOUR CLOOOOSET!" she yelled in a sing songy voice.

"SADIE!"

Kelsie finally looked up from her phone, smirking at whatever Malik sent her. "While y'all handle that, I'm gonna shower in the guest room."

"Don't scar my bathroom sending nudes to your man," Amara called.

Kelsie floated down the hallway. "Your bathroom would be honored."

Sadie's cackle echoed from the master bedroom.

"The both of you need to get out of my house," Amara muttered.

♥

When Amara walked into her bedroom, she wasn't shocked. Sadie had struck. Shirts covered the bed. Heels littered the floor. Dresses hung from the closet door like a fashion crime scene. Sadie stood in the middle of the chaos, rifling through hangers with laser focus.

"Uh... you plan on cleaning this up, right?"

Sadie waved her off without looking. "Mmhmm."

"I'll take that as a no..."

"AHA!" Sadie shrieked like she'd cracked a national code. She yanked a few items from the rack, tossed them onto the bed, grabbed heels in one hand and two clutches in the other.

"Here. Try these."

Amara scanned the options. Sadie clearly had no intention of letting her blend into the background. She held up a long-sleeved, ribbed, backless chestnut-brown dress.

"How about this?"

Sadie pursed her lips. "Hmm... try it with these." She held up strappy heels and gold hoops. "And wear your hair up so he can see your back."

Amara nodded and headed to shower. Halfway through turning on the water she heard Kelsie scream.

She knew that scream.

Sadie had turned on the cold water in the guest room shower. Again.

Amara couldn't help but laugh. She finished getting ready, slipped into the dress, and fastened the gold hoops. She admired her reflection.

She looked damn good.

"Ready?" Kelsie called down the hall.

Amara took one last look in the mirror. She was ready for whatever the night would bring her.

Chapter Fifteen

Amara knew she looked good when her friends whistled and cat-called as she stepped out of her bedroom. But nothing prepared her for the reaction she got walking through the glass doors of The Contemporary Art Studio.

At first she thought the stares were for Kelsie, per usual, until Sadie nudged her.

"Now... did I make you look good, or did I make you look good?"

"You did alright," Amara teased.

"Alright? I should invoice you for how fine you look."

"She's right," Kelsie added. "Your man's gonna be real happy."

"He is not my man. And he's not even here."

"Oh, so you already know who we're talking about," they cackled as Amara shot them a deadly look.

"Let's enjoy the artwork. Can y'all behave for one night?"

They mimed zipping their lips.

The gallery was stunning. Minimalist lighting. Soft shadows. Sculptures glowing like they had their own pulse. One piece made them stop.

A gray clay torso of a woman split down the center. One side darker and weighed down, the other lighter but equally burdened.

"There's so much sorrow in this," Sadie whispered. "Like she's torn between what she survived and what she hopes for."

A low, melodic voice answered behind them.

"It's about heartbreak. And the feeling of stepping into something new before you're sure you're ready."

They turned.

"Hi, I'm Rhiannon."

Ryan's sister was breathtaking. Almond eyes, warm brown skin, an easy smile, sleeves rolled to reveal inked forearms.

Sadie blinked like she'd seen a goddess. Kelsie took a mental note to ask her about her skincare routine. Rhiannon walked them through her pieces with ease and charm, until exaggerated throat clears broke the moment.

"Alright, lil sis, let them breathe."

Ryan.

The sound alone made heat rise low in Amara's body.

"Excuse her," he said. "Rhi can be a lot."

Rhiannon smirked. "I'm just doing my job."

"As a menace," Ryan countered.

She turned to Sadie, eyes twinkling. "What else was I supposed to do with three beautiful women?"

Sadie's blush deepened.

Kelsie fanned herself. "Whew. Is it hot in here?"

Malik slid behind her, arms wrapping around her waist. "Damn, Kels. I can't compete with Rhi."

"You don't need to," she giggled as he kissed her neck.

King appeared instantly, stepping between Rhiannon and Sadie. "Back up. You're always trying to steal somebody's girl."

Sadie blinked. "Whose girl? Where she at?"

Rhiannon looked him up and down. "Looks like that's a one-sided fantasy but go off."

Their bickering became the evening's entertainment.

Ryan placed a hand at the small of Amara's back, and her entire body warmed. "I'm glad you came."

She shrugged lightly. "My girls were free. We needed something to do."

He let his gaze travel over her slowly. "Have I told you how sexy you look in brown?"

Heat shot down her spine.

"You know," she murmured, "I don't think you have."

"Ahem."

Kelsie's throat clear cut through the moment.

"Get a room!" King yelled.

"Are you really yelling in a damn art exhibit?" Sadie scolded.

"Anything to get your attention," King declared to her.

Sadie turned to Rhiannon. "Mind giving me a personal tour, Rhiannon?"

"Call me Rhi." She linked their arms.

"Okay, Rhi." Sadie looked back at King and stuck her tongue out.

King clutched his chest. "She wants me," he proclaimed as he followed her.

"The delusion your cousin has is inspiring," Kelsie whispered to Malik.

"We should follow them."

"We'll come too!" Amara blurted.

"No," the entire group snapped in unison.

Rhiannon laughed. "Ryan's been here since setup. He can give you a private tour."

"Yeah, he got you," Malik added, clapping Ryan's back.

Ryan looked at Amara, dimples deepening. "It's up to you."

Her stomach fluttered. She hadn't felt like this since Marcus. The thought threatened to pull her under, but she inhaled slowly, grounding herself.

Marcus was the past. Ryan the new and maybe even the future.

"Sure," she said, eyes steady on his. "You can be my private tour guide."

Chapter Sixteen

The two of them stood in silence, waiting for the other to make the first move. Amara's pulse kicked hard in her chest. *You can be my private tour guide? Who even says that?*

She could already hear the jokes Sadie and Kelsie were going to unleash later.

Ryan stepped closer and held out his hand like it was the most natural thing in the world, that slow, easy smile forming.

"You ready?" he asked.

Those words transported her back to 3Kings, right before he lifted her onto the pillows and learned her body like a course he wanted to ace.

Her stomach fluttered. Maybe she shouldn't have run out of the studio that day or left him standing in the parking lot shirtless as she peeled off like she was being chased.

She took his hand. His fingers closed around hers, firm and sure, letting her know he was taking lead. They walked slowly through the gallery, pausing at each piece as Ryan talked about Rhiannon's work with a kind of pride that softened her from the inside out. Eventually they wound up in a quieter corner, tucked away from the noise.

He grabbed two glasses of wine from a passing server and nodded toward the exit door.

"Do you still trust me?" he asked, holding it open with one hand.

She lifted a brow. "I'm not sure when the first time was that I trusted you."

He stepped in close, brushing his thumb along the side of her hand. The touch was so small and simple but ruined her.

"We're still pretending like I didn't have your legs wrapped around me," he said quietly.

Her breath caught.

"Or your nails in my back."

She swallowed.

"Or you biting my shoulder the deeper I—"

Her knees dipped. Ryan caught her before she could lose balance, steadying her with both hands. He stepped back, licking his lips like he knew exactly what he was doing to her.

"So again... do you trust me?"

She nodded.

"You know I like when you say it," he murmured, that honeyed Texas accent pouring over her.

Her voice was barely a whisper. "I trust you."

Ryan pushed the door open and led her upstairs.

The rooftop stole the rest of her breath.

String lights hung overhead like stars, warm and golden. A mural of the city stretched along one wall. A fire pit glowed at the center of the space, flames swaying with the breeze.

"This is beautiful," she said.

"I'll let Rhi know you said that."

"The owners hired her to do the mural?"

"She is one of the owners," he said. "When our mom passed, she left each of us money with strict instructions to invest in something we love.

Rhi wrote up this whole plan for a space that spotlighted new artists for free."

"That's incredible," Amara said softly. "Is that how you started the studio too?"

"That and Malik having NFL money helped," he teased. "King put in some. I barely touched what Mom left. Which means...I need something else to invest in. I am thinking of starting a program for young aspiring photographers in low-income areas."

He pointed to the bar. "You want a drink?"

"What do you have?"

"What do you want? Wine? Something stronger? You want me to make something?"

"I didn't know my private tour guide doubled as a bartender."

"I am a man of many talents, AJ. I can be whatever you need."

"AJ?" she asked, smirking.

"Are business colleagues supposed to have nicknames?"

"Colleague?" He clutched his chest dramatically. "Wow. That hurt. I thought I was more than that."

"You told me this was a business meeting."

"So, you wanted it to be more." He leaned closer.

"A cosmo," she said quickly.

"What?"

"That's what I want. A cosmopolitan."

"That's light work."

While he made the drink, she drifted toward the edge of the rooftop. The city hummed below them. The breeze lifted her curls and brushed against the open back of her dress.

"Music?" he asked, handing her the drink.

"That depends. What're you playing?"

"What're you in the mood for?"

"Surprise me."

He grinned. "I'm pretty good at picking the right song."

"You can't brag and not back it up."

"I got you."

He unlocked his phone and let the speakers hum awake.

The sound of swiping filled the air before the speakers settled into the soft pitter-patter of rain, followed by familiar drum taps, a gentle guitar, and smooth vocals of Sade's Sweetest Taboo.

Amara tilted her head back, her hips beginning to sway, legs and shoulders moving in rhythm as the music wrapped around her. Ryan watched in awe, slipping into photographer mode. He pulled out his phone to capture her in that carefree moment.

She paused, heat rising across her cheeks, but kept dancing.

He set his phone down and stepped behind her, hands gliding to her waist, sinking into her rhythm. She leaned back into him, letting the song guide them. It felt like falling into something familiar and brand new all at once.

He turned her toward him and kissed her. She melted into it, fingers curling behind his neck. He kissed her again, then twirled her, laughter spilling between them in the warm night air.

"Let me take you out on a real date," he murmured.

She looked from him, to the firelight flickering around them, to the empty glasses on the ledge.

"Ask me again when we're sober," she said. "And I might say yes."

He leaned in, his hands cupping her face—

A loud vibration ricocheted off the table Amara placed her phone.

Amara groaned. "Sadie's had enough of King."

Ryan blinked. "How do you know?"

Her phone buzzed again.

"And...that's Kelsie."

She grabbed her clutch. "I gotta go."

"Until next time?" he asked.

She laughed softly as she walked toward the stairs. Before stepping through the door, she looked back at him, framed in firelight and city glow.

"Thank you for tonight."

"I'm glad you came."

"Me too."

Chapter Seventeen

Amara woke up to the smell of toast and the soft scratch of a stylus moving across a tablet. Sadie was perched on the couch, sketching while devouring avocado toast like she owned the place.

"Somebody slept in," Sadie murmured without looking up.

"And somebody used every pan I own to make toast," Amara said, stretching.

"I'll clean it up, Mom."

Amara rolled her eyes. "Did Kelsie make it home okay?"

"If by home you mean Malik's place, then yes."

"So, they're really back on, huh?"

"From the way they were acting last night. Absolutely. And they're not the only ones."

"What do you mean?" Amara asked as she opened the fridge.

Sadie shot up, crumbs falling down her lap. "Don't play coy. Where did you disappear to last night? I couldn't find you anywhere in the exhibit."

Amara blushed as she rummaged through the fridge. "Did you use all the tomato?"

"Girl, forget the tomato!" Sadie shut the fridge door with her hip. "Give. Me. The tea."

Ding.

Both women froze.

A notification glowed from the counter.

New message from Ryan H.

New photo from Ryan H.

Sadie lunged for the phone with Olympic-level reflexes.

"Ha!" she cackled, unlocking it before Amara could intercept. Her jaw dropped as she read the message aloud.

The attached photo was of Amara on the rooftop. Her arms raised, curls wild, hips tilted, joy shining through her smile.

"Oh. My. God. You whore. Explain this. Was this last night? What is happening in this photo!?"

Amara snatched her phone back. "I was dancing, okay?"

"Dancing!? Outside!?"

Amara groaned. "Can I eat first?"

Sadie shoved her plate at her. "Here. Eat and spill."

Amara took a bite, chewed, then gave in. She told her everything. Ryan's soft but confident tour, how he bragged about his sister's art, the rooftop surprise, the cosmos, the music, the way he held her hand like it was the most natural thing in the world. By the time she finished, Sadie was a swooning on the couch.

"Aww! You have to text him back."

"I know, but what do I say? I don't want to sound desperate."

"You're spiraling, girl. Give me the phone."

Amara handed it over reluctantly and watched her type with villainous enthusiasm.

"Done," Sadie said, handing it back.

```
Amara: Good morning. Could almost be a
model for your next book cover
```

"SADIE!" Amara shrieked, throwing a pillow at her. Sadie ducked and cackled.

Ding.

They froze again.

```
New message from Ryan H.
```

Sadie yelled from behind the couch, "WHAT DID HE SAY!?"

"Don't you have somewhere to be?" Amara shot back.

"Ugh! Rude." Sadie grabbed her tablet and bag. "I know when I'm not wanted."

"You're ridiculous."

"Love you too!"

The door clicked shut behind her.

Amara stared at her phone, heart thudding. Should she play it cool? Wait? Respond fast?

Stop. Breathe.

She opened the message.

Ryan: I think I can make that happen. What are you up to today?

Amara: Heading to my parents café to help with book club until four. You?

Ryan: Book club? Reading anything I might know?

Amara: Maybe? YA mystery.

The Final Shot Clock.

Ryan: Yeah, never heard of it. We should read it for our next book club.

Amara: When did we join a book club?

Ryan: When you strong-armed me into reading so I could prove I deserved to photograph your birthday.

Amara: Strong-armed!? Dramatic.

Ryan: What would you call it then?

Incoming Call: Mom.

Amara: Can we talk later? My mom will keep calling till I step through the café door.

Ryan: Of course.

♥

Amara tried focusing during book club but spent most of the time smiling at her phone like she was sixteen again. Butterflies. Real, nonstop butterflies.

As she wrapped up the session, anxiety crept in. Should she text him later? Wait a day? Follow Kelsie's rule: be the chased, not the chaser? But what if he didn't text again?

"Ms. Amara?"

She blinked. "Yes, Camila?"

The girl held out the gently buzzing phone. "It's vibrating."

Amara saw the name on the screen and nearly choked.

She picked it up. "Hello?"

"Hey." His voice alone steadied her nerves and made her chest warm. "How was book club?" he asked.

"It was good. I'm walking out now. Were you counting the minutes till I was free?"

She winced. *Too much.*

Ryan laughed. "Oh, so you got jokes."

She laughed too. "How was your day?"

"Pretty straight. But it's about to get better."

"Oh yeah? What's next?"

"That depends on your answer to one question."

"Hm. Okay, I'll bite."

"Would you like to have dinner at my place? Eight o'clock?"

"Well," she said casually, although she was screaming internally. "That depends on how you answer *my* question."

Ryan chuckled. "And what's that, Ms. Jones?"

"Is this a date... or another business meeting?"

His laugh was deep and warm.

"Yes, Ms. Jones. It's a date. Leave the blazer at home."

"Oh man, and I had the perfect power suit picked out."

"Ah! You got jokes?"

Her smile stretched. "How about eight?"

"Eight it is. I'll text you the address."

"See you soon."

Chapter Eighteen

She arrived at his condo on Rose Lane, taking a deep breath before knocking on the door.

Relax, girl. It's just dinner.

The second he opened it, that lie evaporated. Her breath caught. How was it possible for this man to be even finer up close? His freshly oiled beard sharpened the lines of his jaw. The gold chain at his neck drew her eyes down to the definition of his shoulders, the strength of his chest, and the veins in his arms trailing to the fingers she remembered.

He pulled her into a slow, deliberate hug, his hand caressing the small of her back. She melted, silently begging for him to grab her ass. When he didn't, she hated how soon he let go.

"Come in," Ryan said, stepping back. "I have a surprise for you in the kitchen."

"What kind of surprise?"

"You'll see in about thirty seconds." He reached for her hand. She let him take it. She was getting used to this, letting him lead, trusting him without thinking. She could do this forever.

They followed a trail of rose petals.

"Close your eyes," he said.

She obeyed, fingers tightening around him.

"Open."

A bouquet of roses sat in a tall vase on sleek black marble. A bottle of wine and two glasses waited beside it. Ingredients lined the back counter.

"I thought we could cook together," he said.

"From private tours to private cooking lessons. A man of many talents, huh?"

"Don't forget private photo shoots," he murmured against her ear.

She looked up at him, biting her lip. "I could never forget that."

He tilted her chin and kissed her. Soft at first. Too soft. She wanted more, needed it. She deepened the kiss, hunger rising fast. His hands slid down to her ass, gripping each cheek like he wanted to memorize her body. She gasped. *Finally!*

He lifted her effortlessly and sat her on the counter. His mouth trailed down her neck, then lower, tugging her top over her head, revealing her black lace bra. His kisses traced her stomach, unzipping her jeans, sliding them off to reveal matching lace panties.

He dropped to his knees like he was worshipping her. His hands anchored her thighs as he pulled her close. She shuddered the moment his tongue touched her, one hand burying in his hair, the other gripping the counter. She followed the rhythm of his tongue with her clit, back arched until his name escaped her lips.

He kissed her one last time before helping her down.

"Thanks for dessert," he said. "When I get back, we can make dinner."

He disappeared toward the bathroom.

What the hell just happened?

"Someone missed me," she called out.

He laughed. "Just a little."

She cleared her throat, desperate to cool her blush. "So... what's for dinner?"

"Steak medallions, potatoes, and asparagus." He washed his hands. Even watching him wash his hands was a turn on.

"You've made this before, right? Because the most I've ever been trusted with is salad."

"I find that hard to believe."

"No, seriously. My mom barely even trusts me with that."

"Don't worry. I'll show you everything."

She stepped into his space. "Alright, Chef Hartwell. I'm all yours."

They cooked together. Her peeling potatoes badly, him laughing and gently correcting her. She mixed up teaspoons and tablespoons; he didn't let her live it down.

"How about some music?" he asked.

"I'm picking this time. You can't outdo me twice."

"You know your books," he said, grinning, "I know my music. It's my secret weapon."

"We'll see." She slid a vinyl from his collection.

Soon, D'Angelo's Brown Sugar filled the kitchen.

Ryan sang off-key, twirling her around. She joined him, just as off-key. They laughed as they danced their way to dinner.

" *'I know my music'*," she mimicked in a terrible imitation of his voice.

"Yeah, but you used my records!" He rebutted

"And you're a sore loser?"

"Okay, you got me. And you don't back down from a challenge. Noted."

"Something I got from my dad."

"I got my taste in music from mine." His voice softened. "Our house was always full of music. My parents used to sit on the porch every Sunday night and just vibe."

"No wonder you and Rhiannon are so smooth."

"You could say that." He smiled. "My mom had all the game. My dad just tried to keep up."

"She sounds amazing. This steak is amazing too. Where'd you learn to cook?"

"Trial and error. YouTube. Hunger." He chuckled. "After my mom passed, Rhi and I took turns making dinner. Helped us pretend things were normal. My dad... he lost himself for a while."

Amara reached for his hand. "I'm so sorry."

"It's okay. He's doing better." He took a breath. "Anyway. Don't want to get too heavy."

"You're not. Dates are for this stuff. Getting to know each other."

He blinked. "Can you say that again?"

"What?"

"You called this a date. I'm just making sure I heard it right."

"Oh my God, Ryan. Yes. We're on a date."

"LET'S GOOOOO!" he yelled, jumping up.

"Sit down!" She laughed.

"I'm sorry. I just never thought I'd see the day."

"Keep it up and we're going back to business meetings."

"Who's the sore loser now?"

"Shut up. Do you have more wine?"

He got up. "Always."

While he grabbed the bottle, Amara flipped through his records, choosing one more.

Prince. Sound O' the Times.

The smooth croons of Adore filled the room. Ryan returned mouthing the lyrics, pointing at her dramatically. She laughed, swaying her hips. He watched her for a long moment before stepping into her arms.

They danced slowly. His hand at her back. Hers on his chest. She inhaled him, the moment, the feeling of safety and ease. She could've stayed like that forever... until reality nudged her.

"What time is it?" she asked reluctantly.

Ryan checked. "11:28."

"Damn. Seriously?"

"Too late?"

"Actually, yeah. Big day tomorrow. It's Open Mic Night at the café."

"Oh yeah. Ima be there."

"You will?"

"Your mom invited me to shoot the event."

"What?" She blinked.

Obviously I need to have another talk about meddling.

"Is that cool?"

"Yeah. Of course! It's fine."

He helped her into her coat, his fingers brushing her shoulders. At the door, he turned her, pulling her close.

"For the record, I hate that you're leaving."

"Me too." She rose on her toes to kiss him, soft but charged.

"Can I pick you up tomorrow?" he asked.

She nodded. "I need to be there around three."

"That's fine. Send me your address."

"I will," she whispered.

"Goodnight, Ms. Jones."

"Goodnight, Mr. Hartwell."

Chapter Nineteen

Ryan pulled up to Amara's place in his sleek black sports car, right on time. She was already waiting by the curb, curls pinned back in soft waves, wearing a Jones Café sweatshirt and the jeans that made her ass look like Beyonce's.

He had to blink twice. It brought him right back to the first time he ever saw her. He stepped out and opened the passenger door for her with a grin.

"I was going to say you look beautiful, but you already know that."

Amara paused at the door, her gaze softening as she looked up at him. Then, without a word, she rose onto her tiptoes and kissed him, slow and unhurried.

"I'm not gonna stop you from saying it though," she murmured with a smirk and slid into the seat.

As she adjusted herself, her breath caught when he crossed in front of the car, the sunlight catching the sharp cut of his jaw and the easy sway of his walk. Damn. He slid into the driver's seat and stole another glance her way.

She chuckled. "What?"

"You sure you need to be there at three?" he asked, resting a hand on her thigh.

"You are not about to make me late," she said, blushing. "Drive before you get us both in trouble. My mom doesn't play about time."

He started the engine. "You're the boss." But his hand didn't move.

They cruised through the neighborhood, vibing to an R&B playlist while she lazily ran her fingers through his beard. At a red light, he turned toward her, their faces inches apart.

"You're so damn beautiful, Amara." He lifted her hand, laced their fingers, and pressed a kiss to her knuckles.

When they pulled into the café lot, he leaned over and tipped her chin up, their mouths met in a deep, slow kiss. His hand drifted up the nape of her neck, thumb brushing her skin as their lips tangled. Amara moaned softly, slipping her hand under the hem of his shirt to feel his firm core.

Honk!

They broke apart, startled. Kelsie and Sadie sat a few feet back in Sadie's Bronco. Kelsie leaned out the window with a smirk.

"In front of your parents' café though? Brave."

Sadie honked again, playfully shaking her head.

"We're coming!" Amara called out, laughing as she touched up her lip gloss and tucked it back into her purse.

Ryan circled around and opened her door. "Looks like we're busted."

"We weren't even doing anything," she said as she stepped out.

"Yet," he muttered under his breath.

They walked toward the entrance hand in hand.

Open Mic Night had become a staple at the Jones Café. The line wrapped around the building, people swaying to music drifting from inside. Young couples leaned against the brick wall, laughing between kisses, while groups of friends snapped selfies under the glow of the streetlights.

Inside, guitarists tuned, poets scribbled last minute edits, and singers murmured melodies to themselves.

They were greeted by the matriarch.

"Oh!" Mrs. Jones looked between them. "I see you've found my surprise... by surprising me."

Amara tilted her head. "Sometimes I can handle my love life on my own, Mom."

"We see that," Sadie interjected. "Ryan, can we steal our friend for a second?"

"For sure. Mrs. Jones, where would you like me to set up?"

Kelsie grabbed Amara's arm, pulling her and Sadie toward the host stand.

"Bitch! Spill," Kelsie demanded.

"Alright, alright. We may or may not have had a date last night."

"Date!?" her friends screamed in unison, startling a nearby server.

Amara caught them up on one of the best dates of her life.

"You've been sitting on this all morning?" Sadie shrieked. "No text? No smoke signal? Nothing?"

"Sadie, chill," Kelsie said, then turned back to Amara. "But seriously... when were you planning to tell us? You know we're Team Ryan."

"One, I wasn't expecting to see him again this fast. Two, my mom invited him. And three... I didn't want to tell y'all until I knew for sure this is something I want."

"Well?" Sadie whispered. "Is it?"

Amara nodded. "I think so."

They screamed again.

Before she could say anything else, Mrs. Jones clapped from across the room.

"Alright everyone! Places! Doors are opening!"

The café filled quickly with patrons. People took their seats, placed orders, browsed through the books and records. The artists lined up in the corner as the owners stepped onto the stage, welcoming the crowd and announcing the night's community partner.

One by one, performers mesmerized the room. Applause and snaps filled the air. Then the final performer stepped up.

"My name is Devaughan and I want to slow it down a bit."

The performer strummed the opening chords of a familiar tune. A slow, stripped-down acoustic version of Sweetest Taboo. It was starting to feel like this was their song. Though they stood on opposite sides of the room, the moment their eyes met, it was as if no distance separated them. Ryan lowered his gaze to his camera and began taking pictures of Amara. She ached for him to be close enough for a kiss. She set down the notepad she'd been using to take orders, her focus narrowing on him.

Before she could even think about it, she was moving towards him. She took the camera from his hands, setting it aside without a word. Her fingers trembled as they slid around the back of his neck. Her lips crashed into his, full of fire and urgency. Sparks ignited as the song soared into its climatic bridge. She knew more than ever that this is what she wanted. *He* is who she wanted.

Devaughan strummed the final chord as the crowd erupted into applause, but she barely heard it. All she could feel was the press of Ryan's lips on hers, the fire still burning low and steady in her chest as she stepped back.

They didn't say a word. Everything that needed to be said had already been left between their lips. They stood still for a long moment, until the applause drew them back to the room. Amara gave him a soft smile before slipping away, heart pounding. There was still a shift to finish, and the night wasn't over, but something between them had changed.

♥

As the café emptied and the night wound down, Ryan stayed behind to help clean up. He broke down the stage with her father, stealing glances at Amara wiping down the counter. He could still feel her mouth on his.

"So what do you think?" Jerome's voice cut in.

"Huh?" Ryan blinked. "Sorry... what?"

"Sunday dinner at our place. We'll watch the playoffs. I'm making chili. You can bring friends if you want. And you can even continue to stare at my daughter, if you like."

Ryan flushed. "Sorry, sir. Sunday works. What time?"

"Game starts at four. Come around three."

"Thanks, sir."

"Call me Jerome."

They stacked the last chairs. Ryan looked toward the front of the café. Amara was waiting by the door. She was the sweetest taboo.

Chapter Twenty

The living room buzzed with laughter and football commentary as Mr. Jones, Sadie, Ryan and his friends leaned into the game. The air was thick with the scent of chili and cornbread drifting in from the kitchen. Somehow, Sadie and King were getting along, proving football and chili could work miracles.

Kelsie, Amara, and Mrs. Jones joined the group in the living room.

"I'm gonna check on the chili." Mr. Jones announced.

Kelsie slid into the seat beside Malik, leaning into him like it was second nature. Sadie and Amara exchanged a look, smirking. They had never seen Kelsie this soft with anyone.

Sadie whispered, "Looks like someone broke the three month curse. You should be over there with your man too."

Amara didn't argue. She moved to Ryan's side of the room and slipped her arms around his waist, molding her body into the strength of his back, catching the faint scent of bergamot from his hoodie.

"Hey," she murmured. "I'm glad you came."

He took her hands gently into one of his, his thumb tracing slow, soothing circles over her wrists.

"Me too."

Then the worst possible thing happened.

Marcus's face filled the TV screen, grinning through a locker room interview.

"...my new recruit? Kid's a beast. No one's touching him."

Sadie stiffened, chip frozen halfway to her mouth. "Turn it off," she snapped. "Now."

Mrs. Jones swooped in. "Dinner's ready."

The guys exchanged confused glances. King looked at Mr. Jones. "What was that about?"

Jerome's jaw tightened. "Just like Marcus to ruin a nice afternoon."

"It's okay, Daddy," Amara said quickly, forcing a smile. But Ryan caught the flash of pain in her eyes. "I'll get the bowls out."

"I'll help," her mother offered.

"Alone. I got it. It's fine."

She disappeared down the hall quietly slipping into the bathroom instead. She shut the door gently, gripping the sink with both hands as she stared into the mirror.

Don't cry. Not today. Not in front of them.

He always managed to creep back in. Through screens, through people, through happy moments. Always when she was finally feeling whole again and building something with someone new.

She steadied her breathing, wiped the tears from her face, and splashed cool water on it. Ryan met her gaze when she opened the door. Ryan stood there, hands tucked in the pocket of his hoodie, worry softening his features.

"You alright, AJ?" he asked gently.

She nodded. Then she shook her head. "No. Not really."

"Wanna step outside?"

She nodded again.

Out on the patio, the cool air gave her lungs room to breathe. The sun was dipping low, casting warm light across the side of the house. She leaned against the railing, arms crossed tightly.

"I didn't expect to see his face today," she said quietly. "He still gets to me... more than I'd like to admit."

Ryan stayed silent, letting her speak.

"He didn't just cheat," she whispered, voice cracking. "He cheated with my roommate. We'd been together for years. I thought we were building something, but on my birthday..." She swallowed hard. "Everything changed after that. And now he gets to be this golden agent everyone loves. No one knows the real him."

His jaw flexed. He wanted to pull up to the stadium and beat Marcus's ass. He wanted to erase every bruise that he left on her heart. But he stayed calm.

"People like that love to rewrite the story," he said. "Especially when they're the villain."

That earned a small, broken laugh.

"But just so we're clear," he added, "anyone who hurts someone as special as you aren't very smart."

Her smile was fragile.

"And that roommate?" Ryan continued. "I KNOW she's not as fine as you."

That pulled out a real laugh, warm and loud.

"You're ridiculous."

"Nah," he said, nudging her shoulder. "I'm observant."

He let the moment breathe.

"Dinner's probably ready."

"Yeah," she said, straightening. "Let's go eat."

After their bellies were full and cheeks numb from laughing, Amara stood with Ryan by the front door. Her family's voices echoed behind them, but out here it felt quiet.

"I'll walk you out," she said.

They stepped down the walkway together, walking at a synchronized pace. When they reached his car, he turned to her with an easy smile, the porch light catching his dimple.

"Thanks for dinner. Your dad might've outdone himself with that chili."

"I'll tell him. He loves the attention."

Ryan chuckled softly.

"Well…" Amara looked up at him, biting her lip. "Goodnight."

He wrapped his arms around her waist and kissed her like he didn't want to let go. He was really falling for her.

"I feel like I need to redeem myself from earlier." She smirked. "Let me take you somewhere fun."

"Fun? What do you have in mind?"

"What are you doing Saturday afternoon?"

"I'm trying to see what's fun for you, AJ?"

"You'll see."

Ryan watched her walk away, her curls bouncing with every step, the porch light softening the curve of her silhouette. Whatever she had planned for Saturday, he didn't care.

As long as she was there, he was in.

Chapter Twenty-One

Ryan pulled into the lot outside the trail park and spotted Amara by the entrance. Even in leggings, a cropped hoodie, and sneakers, she looked effortless. Maybe the most beautiful he'd ever seen her. He would never have guessed that ATV riding was her idea of fun, but he was all for it.

"You ready to get smoked?" she asked, smirk sharp enough to cut.

He laughed. "You probably don't even know how to start one of these."

"Well prepare to be shocked, Ryan. I am a Jane of all trades."

They walked toward the rental booth, signed waivers, listened to the rundown, then mounted their ATVs. Amara yelped when hers roared to life, the vibration jolting her forward.

Ryan grinned. "Don't worry. I'll go easy on you."

"You better not!" She gunned the throttle and tore off.

The trail wound through a stretch of Georgia woods, leaves crunching beneath the tires as they carved through the path. Cold air nipped at their cheeks, but adrenaline made it feel like nothing.

Ryan tried keeping up, but Amara was a menace behind the handlebars. Grinning through her tinted goggles, whooping as she hit a bump, kicking up dirt behind her.

"You trying to leave me in the dust, AJ?" he shouted over the roar.

She slowed just enough to toss him a look. "If you can't keep up, just say that!"

They rounded a curve and coasted to a stop beside a small clearing framed by towering trees. Amara removed her helmet, curls wild, smile brighter than the sun cutting through the branches.

Ryan climbed off his ATV, still breathless. "Okay, okay. You got it. I'm officially humbled."

She laughed, breath puffing in the cool air. "Told you you'd be shocked."

He walked closer, gaze traveling slowly over her wind-kissed cheeks and flushed lips. "You're unreal. You know that?"

She raised an eyebrow. "For beating your ass?"

"No." He stepped closer. "For looking sexy as hell doing it."

Her cheeks warmed as she tried to hide her smile.

"You hungry? There's a little farm stand nearby. Cider, donuts, things to warm you up."

Ryan grinned. "You had me at donuts."

Hours later, full of hot cider and sugar-dusted donuts, they stood by Ryan's car, sharing long, slow, teenager-style kisses. Every time they pulled apart, they went right back in. Amara brushed her thumb along his jaw.

"You wanna come back to my place?"

His brow lifted. "Yeah?"

"Yeah," she whispered, biting her lip. "You can swing by your place first and grab a few things."

"Cool. I'll be quick."

He kissed her one last time before walking to his car. Amara waited until he turned the corner, then spun toward hers. She texted him asking to give her at least an hour, then rushed to her car.

♥

She quickly entered her home and headed straight for the shower. Afterward, she smoothed vanilla body butter over her skin, the kind that melted in and left her smelling like sin wrapped in sweetness.

She slipped into a soft nude chemise debating between keeping her hair up or letting her hair down. She opted to let her curls fall...for now. Candles flickered in the living room and down the hall. A slow, sultry playlist pulsed through the house. Her favorite throw blanket, usually folded neatly on the couch, was stretched across the foot of her bed.

She checked her reflection one last time, reapplying her gloss for the fifth time and exhaled before opening the door for Ryan.

"Hey," he said, voice lower than usual.

"Hey," she replied, matching his energy.

He dropped his bag and pulled her in, kissing her like it had been days instead of hours. He moved his hands up her thighs, finding the part of her that responded instantly to his touch.

"Ryan..." she gasped as his thumb circled her most sensitive spot.

He lifted her with ease, her legs wrapping around his waist, as he carried her to the couch and laying her down like she was something precious.

He dropped to his knees, ready to please her.

"Wait," Amara breathed.

He froze. "You okay? We don't have to rush anything. Say the word and I'll stop."

She nodded, then wrapped her arms around his neck. "I'm okay, baby. I want this. But you always take care of me. Let me take care of you tonight."

She rose from the couch, guiding him down. A hair tie on the coffee table slid onto her wrist. She tied her curls back and slid his pants down mouthwatering at the sight of his length. Long, thick, ready for her. She traced it with her tongue slowly and purposefully. Her hands stroked the base as her mouth took him deeper. His breath stuttered.

"Shiiit, Amara!"

She moaned in approval, increasing the pressure, loving how he sounded when he unraveled. When he finally released with a choked groan, she swallowed every bit of his pleasure. Then kissed his stomach, chest, neck, guiding him to the bedroom for round two.

"Shirt. Off. Now," she said.

He obeyed instantly. Normally, he gave the orders, but tonight? She wanted to lead. Her chemise dropped to the floor.

"Lay back. I'm not done taking care of you yet." She straddled his waist, sinking down onto him with a soft, broken moan. Her hands pressed to his chest as she set the rhythm, slowly allowing him to fill her up. His hands gripped her hips, guiding her, losing himself in her, until they came undone together. Soft kisses carried them to sleep.

Chapter Twenty-Two

Amara lay curled into Ryan's side, her leg tangled with his, her cheek pressed to the warm rise of his chest. Neither of them moved. The room was warm and quiet, suspended in that in-between space where the world hadn't started yet.

"We should get up," Ryan murmured, brushing his lips across her forehead.

"We should," she echoed sleepily. "How do you feel about brunch?"

He smiled, eyes still closed. "I know exactly what to make."

She lifted her head and arched a brow. "You know all this cooking is going to spoil me?"

"That's the point." He kissed her forehead.

Amara tucked herself closer, grinning. She could've stayed there forever, wrapped in his warmth and the steady beat of his heart, but Ryan was already sitting up.

"I'll go shower then get started," he said, voice rough from sleep. "You rest. You were working overtime last night."

She rolled her eyes as he left the room, but the smile stayed.

She considered joining him, her body still humming from the night before, but she was deliciously sore in the best way. Her legs weren't even pretending to cooperate. Her body demanded sleep, and she surrendered.

♥

The smell of cinnamon and vanilla pulled her awake. She hopped into the shower, slipped into his hoodies, and padded into the kitchen.

Ryan stood at the stove in sweatpants, barefoot and shirtless, whisking batter in time with the rain tapping the windows. If she wasn't careful, she could really fall for this man.

"Staring is rude," he said without turning around.

"Cooking in sweats is rude," she shot back, settling on a stool. "Some of us are still recovering from last night."

He laughed quietly. "Coffee?"

"Yes, please. And French toast. And maybe a kiss."

He brought her a mug, leaned down, and kissed her slow enough to warm her straight through. After they ate, they curled under a shared blanket on the couch while an overly cheerful Christmas movie played. Amara rolled her eyes every ten minutes. Ryan cracked jokes every five. Somehow, by the second act, they were fully invested.

"I swear if she doesn't kiss him before the gingerbread competition, I'm turning this off," Amara muttered.

"Patience," Ryan teased, tightening his arm around her shoulders. "Love takes time."

"He built her a sleigh out of barn wood scraps. That man deserves commitment."

Ryan burst out laughing. "Look at you. Getting mad about fake snow love stories."

She snuggled deeper into him. "I like this."

He glanced down, voice soft. "What, the sleigh?"

"No." She traced a slow circle on his chest. "This. Being here with you."

He held her tighter, pressed a long kiss to her temple, and let the rain and the movie fill the quiet.

"Yeah," he murmured. "Me too."

By late afternoon she was asleep again, curled against him, her breath soft against his chest. Ryan ran his fingers through her curls like he was learning her curl pattern by heart.

He didn't want to leave. But he had a sunrise shoot in the Blue Ridge Mountains. He woke her with soft kisses, she blinked up at him, pout and all.

"You're leaving?" she whispered.

"I'll be back," he said against her lips. "Promise."

They walked to the door, both dragging their feet.

"Let me know when you get home," she murmured.

"I will."

The soundtrack of rain and 2000s R&B accompanied him on his drive home. But his thoughts were louder. He replayed everything in his mind. Her smile pressed to his chest. The way she teased him. How she looked in his hoodie. How naturally she fit beside him. This wasn't just a situationship. Not to him.

By the time he reached his condo, he knew exactly what he wanted to do. He dropped his overnight bag by the door, grabbed a bottle of water, and opened a message thread.

Ryan: Just got in.

Ryan: I miss you already.

Amara: I miss you too. Goodnight

He stared at the screen, heart thudding. He opened a new text thread.

Ryan: Need your help. Want to plan something for Amara. Like… one of those big-ass gestures from corny Christmas movies. You in?

Kelsie: I'm listening…

Rhi: That's what I'm talking about big
bro!

Sadie: *You know she'll kill you if
it's too cheesy. But I'm in*

King: *Bet. I'll grab a bowtie*

Malik: *Anything for my baby's friend*

Kelsie: *Aww Malik*

Ryan grinned at his phone.

He couldn't wait to show Amara just how serious
he was.

Chapter Twenty-Three

Amara woke up floating.

Ryan's scent lingered in her sheets. His goodnight text still glowed at the top of her screen. She hugged her pillow, smiling into the cotton, her heart full from the day before. She felt safe, wanted, and soft. Feelings she hadn't let herself hold in a long time.

Even with a packed day ahead, she drifted through her morning in a dreamlike haze. She hummed while making coffee, grinned at her own reflection, and breezed through her inbox, pausing only to reply to the flood of texts from her friends demanding to know why she skipped Sunday dinner.

Amara: Details coming soon. Just
        know…it was everything.

Ryan's name lit up her phone the moment she hit send.

Ryan: Blue Ridge Mountains giving me
inspiration. Thinking about you… What
do you think about these shots for
that book I told you about?

Amara's pulse fluttered.

Amara: Thinking about you too.
And these? They're all amazing.
Impossible to choose.

Ryan: Would it be easier to choose
over dinner tonight?

She didn't even hesitate.

Amara: Yes.

She stared at her screen longer than she meant to, a slow smile spreading. She'd forgotten how sweet the honeymoon stage could be. How light everything felt when someone genuinely wanted you. She didn't feel anxious or guarded.

Nothing could ruin this moment. She leaned over her desk, adjusting the final details of a client proposal, when her phone vibrated again.

```
Chloe (Cleo's Sister): She's in
labor!! At the hospital now.
```

Amara gasped, already grabbing her purse. Thankfully, her team was finishing the final touches on the nursery. She messaged them quickly, letting them know she'd meet them after picking up a gift for the baby.

She headed downtown to her favorite boutique—the one with organic sets that smelled like lavender and dreams. Inside, she moved slowly through the aisles, fingertips grazing soft onesies and hand-stitched blankets. She built the perfect gift basket: a plush animal, a baby journal, a muslin swaddle in warm earth tones. For the last touch, she added tiny camel-colored booties. The perfect baby basket! She made her way to the registered and paused at a familiar figure.

Rebekah.

Tall. Glowing. Very pregnant. Her locs swept to one side, her makeup soft and warm. She looked... settled. Happy, even.

Before Amara could breathe, a familiar laugh drifted from behind her and her chest tightened. The perfect morning she was having, was gone in an instant.

Chapter Twenty-Four

"Hey Bek, look at this."

Marcus's voice carried across the boutique as he lifted a giraffe-print onesie.

Amara froze.

Her stomach dropped.

She ducked behind a rack of little jackets, heart hammering, breath caught in her throat. She hadn't seen them since that birthday. Since the day Rebekah and Marcus blew her life apart.

She scanned the store for an employee, anyone she could hand this basket to so she could leave unnoticed.

No luck.

"Amara!? Amara Jones? Is that you?"

Too late.

Amara closed her eyes, exhaled, and painted on a smile before turning.

"Oh my God, Rebekah Carmichael? It's been ages. How've you been?"

Her voice was steady, but her stomach churned. Playing nice with the woman who helped ruin her life felt like swallowing glass. Marcus didn't even acknowledge her. Still scrolling through baby pajamas like a coward.

Rebekah didn't notice the tension. She kept on, glowing and chatty, talking about baby names and nursery colors like they were old college friends catching up.

This bitch. The audacity.

Amara gave a polite nod, barely hearing anything until something glinted on Rebekah's left hand.

A ring.

Her ring!

The oval-cut diamond on a platinum band. The exact ring Amara had described in their dorm room. The one she told Marcus she wanted someday.

Apparently, he remembered.

Just... not for her.

She swallowed hard.

"You know what, Bek? I should get going," Amara said lightly, lifting the baby basket. "Need to drop this off to a client."

"Of course! So great seeing you!"

Amara forced a smile, walked to the register, paid, and left without looking back.

She reached her car and sank into the driver's seat. The gift basket sat on the passenger side, tiny camel-colored booties peeking out from the tissue paper.

She gripped the steering wheel. It didn't hurt because she wanted him back, *God no*. It hurt because it felt like watching someone else live the version of her life she was supposed to have once upon a time.

The grief of almosts. The anger of having done everything right and still being the one left alone to rebuild. She drove the basket to Cleo's house and handed it to her assistant.

"Leave it on the crib when the team's done. Tell Cleo I'll come by later this week."

"You're not staying?" her assistant asked.

Amara shook her head. "Something came up."

She drove home in silence. A familiar, hollow ache pressing into her ribs.

Inside, she dropped her keys, poured a heavy glass of wine, and sank onto the couch, staring out her massive windows as dusk settled.

Her phone buzzed.

```
Ryan: Is it bad that all I can think
about is seeing your smile tonight?
```

She closed her eyes.

As bad as she wanted to see him, she couldn't show up like this. Not for him. Not when he deserved her whole, not hollow. She typed a short excuse, turned on Do Not Disturb, and set her phone face-down.

Tonight, it would be her, a glass of Chardonnay, and the quiet she knew too well.

Chapter Twenty-Five

Ryan had secured the rooftop at Rhiannon's studio. This time, it would be covered in candles and flowers with soft lights strung across the railings. Rhi was painting a custom mural as the backdrop. He wanted Amara surrounded by beauty. He wanted her to feel like this night was hers. Like it could be theirs.

He even called Mrs. Jones to ask what flowers Amara loved as a kid. Her mom sounded suspicious but charmed and promised not to tell a soul.

Sadie and Kelsie had the duty of getting Amara there without raising suspicion. Everything was coming together. Except one thing.

Amara hadn't said a word.

He'd been texting her small jokes and sweet messages, but nothing came back. At first, he shrugged it off. She was probably buried in client calls. Or with family. Or maybe her phone died.

But by six o'clock, the unease settled in. By seven, he tried one more message.

Still nothing.

He sat alone on the rooftop with the playlist humming low, candles flickering, and the table set for two. His phone finally buzzed.

```
Amara: Can't make it. Sorry.
```

His stomach dropped.

♥

She didn't hear the doorbell the first time.

Or the second.

The third ring rattled straight through her.

"Amaraaaa, open the door!" Sadie's voice boomed.

"Mara, we know you're in there. We can't keep your surprise waiting," Kelsie added.

She cracked the door open, wrapped in a blanket like armor.

Both women froze.

"Girl…" Sadie whispered. "What happened?"

Kelsie stepped inside, her expression shifting from confusion to concern.

Amara sank into a dining chair. Her friends surrounded her without hesitation. And that was all it took. Her composure crumbled. Tears poured in waves she couldn't control.

"I saw Rebekah," she managed between sobs. "And Marcus."

Sadie's mouth fell open. "Where?"

"In a baby store. She's pregnant. And engaged." Amara let out a sharp, bitter laugh. "With the exact ring I told him I wanted in college."

Both friends went still.

"Mara…" Kelsie murmured, rubbing her back.

"I don't want him," Amara rushed out. "I'm not jealous. It just... hit me. Hard. Like the breakup was happening all over again."

Sadie squeezed her hand. "Of course it did. That was trauma."

"And I feel stupid for spiraling," Amara whispered. "I canceled on Ryan tonight."

"That's why we're here," Kelsie said gently. "Now I know why he's blowing up our phones."

Amara winced, guilt settling like a stone in her chest.

Her friends exchanged a look.

"Not sure if this is the right time to tell you this," Sadie said slowly, "but Ryan had something planned tonight."

"Planned?" Amara blinked.

"Like rooftop, flowers, chef, playlist," Kelsie listed. "He was going to make it official tonight."

Her breath caught. "You're lying."

"We wish we were," Sadie said.

Before Amara could speak, the doorbell rang again.

Kelsie checked the peephole. "Oh wow."

She returned with a white bakery box tied with string and a single balloon floating above it.

The note read:

```
I don't know what I did
      but I'm sorry.
Let me make it right.
      - Ryan
```

Amara wallowed as she pressed the note to her chest.

"He didn't even do anything wrong," she whispered. "I'm such a mess."

Sadie nudged her phone toward her. "Then call him. Tell him the truth."

Hands trembling, Amara tapped his name.

He answered on the first ring.

"Hey," he said, hopeful and careful all at once.

"Hey," she breathed. "I got the cookies. And the balloon."

He let out a small chuckle, though it didn't soften his tone. "Wasn't sure if that was too much."

"It wasn't." Her voice wavered. "Ryan... I just... I think I need some space."

Silence. Heavy enough to feel.

"Did I do something?" he asked quietly.

"No. You've been amazing. More than that." Her eyes shut tight. "I just need to breathe."

A long exhale. Then—

"Alright," he said. "If that's what you need."

"It is. It's not about you."

"You said that already."

Her heart sank. "Ryan—"

"It's fine, Amara," he murmured. "Take the space."

She swallowed hard. "Thank you."

"Goodnight."

The line went dead.

Amara lowered her phone, tears sliding down her cheeks as the words slipped out in a whisper meant for no one.

"I think I just lost him."

Kelsie and Sadie wrapped their arms around her, holding her steady, holding her up, holding the pieces together until she could do it herself.

Chapter Twenty-Six

It had been a week.

Seven days without a real conversation. Amara's voice had been replaced by vague texts until they were nothing at all. Ryan kept replaying their last call.

"I just need space right now. It's not you. I promise. I just need some time."

Now he sat at Malik's poker table, barely touching his cards, nursing a bourbon, pretending to follow the trash talk around him. Normally he'd be in it with them, talking shit like always, but he didn't have it in him tonight.

Kelsie walked in mid-game wearing jeans and heels, catching quick glances from every man in the room, but her eyes were locked on Malik.

She wrapped her arms around him and kissed him. The table erupted in jeers. Malik ate it up, pulling her closer and telling everyone how they wished they could get a woman like her.

Kelsie grinned, then spotted Ryan slumping in the corner. After stealing a wing off Malik's plate, she walked over and sat on the arm of the couch beside him.

"You look like shit," she said casually.

Ryan huffed a laugh. "Great to see you too, Kels."

"Amara?"

He rubbed a hand over his jaw. "Nothing."

"Still?"

"She answered once. Said she needed more time. But she didn't sound like herself," he leaned back. "I've been trying to respect that, but I keep thinking maybe I did something wrong."

Kelsie studied him for a beat, jaw tightening like she was holding back what she really wanted to say.

"You didn't. Trust me."

He let out a slow breath. "She's just... different. One minute we're waking up tangled in each other, making French toast, clowning those corny movies. And now? I can't get more than a sentence."

"Ryan," she said gently. "That girl's been through hell. Healing is messy. And sometimes something from the past pops up and knocks the wind out of you."

His eyes narrowed. "So, this is about Marcus? She still has feelings for him?"

"Hell no!" Kelsie said immediately. "Not even close. She's just processing some things."

He stared down at his drink. "I just miss her. And it's not the sex or the cute shit. She makes everything feel lighter. I didn't even know I needed that until she gave it to me."

Kelsie nudged his knee. "You're a good man. She knows that, even if she's drowning in her thoughts right now."

"So what do I do?" he asked quietly.

"You wait," she said. "She cares about you a lot. She's just scared. Give her space to find her way back."

Ryan nodded slowly. "I can do that. Thanks, Kels."

She gave him a warm smile. "No problem. It's still Team Ryan over here."

Chapter Twenty-Seven

Two Weeks Later

It had been two weeks too long since Ryan had seen Amara, heard the song in her laugh, felt the warmth of her touch, or tasted her lips. And today, of all days, he could've used every bit of that.

It was his mother's birthday.

Every year, he and his family honored her, and this year was no different. The scent of cinnamon and butter hit him the moment he walked into his childhood home.

"She's been at it since sunrise," his dad said from the kitchen. "Rhi thinks she can out-toast your mama."

Rhiannon grinned as she flipped a slice in the skillet. "I'm just saying, mine might almost be better than hers. And I used oat milk, so it's healthier."

"French toast ain't supposed to be healthy," their father said, pouring coffee. "Your mother would haunt this whole house if she heard that nonsense."

Ryan smiled, even with the ache in his chest.

♥

Later that morning, they visited the cemetery. They refreshed the flowers and shared their favorite stories, laughing softly through the hurt. Ryan lingered long after the others stepped away, watching the wind stir the trees. Seeing his mother's name etched in granite still didn't feel real.

Back home, they curled up in the living room and pulled out old VHS tapes. The family favorite was the wedding video. The moment the camera caught his mom resting her head on his dad's shoulder during their first dance never failed to hush the room.

"You know your mom almost didn't marry me?" their dad said.

Rhiannon turned. "Wait, what?"

"Mmhmm. Dumb argument. I can't even remember what started it. Something about socks, I think. We stopped speaking for weeks. Then one morning I went to a diner on Peachtree, tried their French toast, and it tasted like cardboard soaked in syrup."

He chuckled, eyes drifting. "I left that place, ran four miles to her parents' house, knocked on the door, breathin heavy, and begged her to take me back."

Ryan laughed. "Because of French toast?"

His father met his eyes. "Because I realized something that morning. I never wanted anybody else's French toast but your mother's."

Silence settled thick and warm over the room.

"When you know something's good," his dad added, "when you know she's the one... you'll do anything to get that back."

Ryan looked away, swallowing hard.

His father had just said the thing he'd been too afraid to admit.

184

If it came down to it, he'd run miles for Amara too.

♥

The sun was setting when Amara stepped into the event space. Two days before her 30th birthday party and everything was ready, except her.

Sadie met her at the door, clipboard in hand, iced macchiato raised like a peace offering. "Lightings fixed. Warm amber. Florals arrive tomorrow. Baby, this space is giving Cupid Bash 2.0."

Amara tried to smile. "Thanks for handling all this."

Sadie studied her. "You sure you're okay?"

"I'm fine," she lied.

They walked through the room together. Champagne sheers over the windows, plush lounge seating, soft R&B drifting through the speakers. Everything looked perfect.

Then they reached the photo wall.

Black-and-white shots suspended in acrylic. Intimate, candid images only he could've taken. Her dancing on Rhi's rooftop. Laughing in satin at 3Kings. Curled in his bed reading, sunlight painting her skin. Pictures only Ryan could have taken.

Her breath stuttered. "I can't do this."

"Mara—"

"I can't do this party without him." Her voice cracked. "I've tried to act fine. But I miss him. Every day. Every minute. It hurts."

Sadie reached for her. "Then go to him."

Amara pulled out her keys. "I'm getting Ryan back."

She headed for the door, wiping her tears, and flung it open.

There Ryan stood. The rain dripping from his hoodie, breath unsteady like he'd run the whole way there.

"I ONLY WANT YOUR FRENCH TOAST!"

Amara blinked. "What?"

He huffed a laugh. "Something my dad said. But I mean it. It's you. You're the one I want.

These past weeks without you? Torture. I don't want space if it means space from you."

His gaze softened. "Let me in, AJ. Whatever you're scared of, we'll handle it together."

Her breath caught. The room blurred until it was only him. Her keys slipped from her hand and hit the floor.

She grabbed him by the hoodie and kissed him like she'd been holding her breath for weeks and he was her air.

Sadie clapped behind them. "About damn time."

Chapter Twenty-Eight

Amara led Ryan to the rooftop terrace. The city stretched beneath them, the hum of Atlanta filling the quiet between them.

"I was scared," she said finally. "Not of you. Of what loving you could cost me."

Her fingers twisted together, and Ryan gently took her hand, steadying her.

"I ran into Rebekah and Marcus the day I went ghost." Her voice wavered. "They looked so happy. Rebekah acted like nothing happened. Like she didn't help destroy my life. Then I saw the ring. The one I described to him in college." She shook her head, breath catching. "It sent me right back to the worst version of myself and reminded me how easy it was for someone I trusted to break me."

She swallowed. "And then there's you. Good and kind and consistent. Everything I wanted but wasn't sure I deserved. I realized how much I was falling for you, and I panicked. My heart was opening again and it terrified me. I froze. I didn't want to feel that hurt again."

Ryan listened without interrupting, jaw tight, eyes soft. When she finished, he stepped closer.

"You could have told me," he said gently. "I would've listened. I wouldn't have judged you. The way you opened up at Sunday dinner... you think I'd ever hold your fear against you?"

He brushed a curl from her face.

"I wish I was there when you saw them, so they could see exactly what they threw away. But hear me on this, Amara. I am not Marcus. I will never hurt you. I'm not going anywhere unless you tell me to."

A laugh slipped out of her, soft and shaky. "Even when I'm a mess?"

He cupped her face, his thumbs warm against her cheeks. "Especially when you're a mess."

She melted into his chest, letting every wall she'd been holding up fall down.

♥

Two nights later, they arrived at her birthday party hand in hand.

The venue glowed in soft blush tones and flickering candlelight. Plush brown accents, champagne drapery, and warm amber uplighting wrapped the room in luxury. She had planned every detail, but tonight none of it mattered.

What mattered was the way Ryan's thumb traced circles on the back of her hand. The way he kept checking on her, how he looked at her.

Her parents swayed in the center of the dance floor, her mom giggling like a girl in love, her dad holding her like he had no plans to let go. Sadie was radiant in green satin, curls framing her face, while Rhiannon whispered something that made her laugh. King hovered closely, planning his next move.

Ryan leaned in. "Sadie might start a civil war before the night ends."

Amara laughed. "She lives for it."

Kelsie and Malik moved in their own rhythm nearby. Amara and Sadie exchanged a glance. Malik had officially broken the 3 month curse.

The music shifted into a slow jam. Ryan pulled her close, hands steady at her waist.

"I love you," he murmured against her temple.

A smile lifted her lips. "I love you, too."

The room swayed around them. Laughter. Music. Friends. Family. Every corner blooming with love. Amara pressed her cheek to Ryan's chest, breathing him in, letting herself settle.

Love was finally in focus.

Acknowledgements

To God. Thank You for the vision, the discipline to finish, and the grace to trust the process even when doubt whispered louder than confidence. Every word exists because You allowed me to see it through.

To my family, my mom and my brothers, thank you for believing in me before the world ever could. Your encouragement, patience, and constant reminders to keep going carried me through every chapter.

To my daughter, Kacee, this is for you. May this always remind you that you can do anything you choose, no matter the timing, the season, or how long the dream takes to unfold.

To my friends, my village, you know who you are. Thank you for listening to ideas out loud, reading drafts, hyping me up when I needed it most, and reminding me that rest is part of the work. This book has pieces of our conversations tucked between the pages.

Lexi and Maya, thank you for standing beside me through it all. Addison, thank you for covering me in prayer, encouragement, and love, and for giving me the push when I needed it most. Devin, thank you for not letting me give up when I was standing at the finish line.

To my ARC team, thank you for your early support, thoughtful feedback, and belief in this story before it ever reached the world. Your encouragement mattered more than you know.

Thank you to Kameelah Pope for bringing my vision to life so beautifully and creating a cover that captures the heart of this story.

To every woman who has loved deeply, been disappointed, healed quietly, and tried again, this story is for you. Your resilience inspired Amara's journey more than you'll ever know.

And to the readers, thank you for choosing this story, for seeing yourselves in these characters, and for supporting my voice. I hope Love In Focus reminds you that love, when it's right, sees you clearly.

Until next time,

J.S. Young

Kelsie's story is coming.....